Pyjamas Are Forgiving

Pyjamas Are Forgiving

Twinkle Khanna

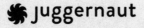

JUGGERNAUT BOOKS

KS House, 118 Shahpur Jat, New Delhi 110049, India

First published by Juggernaut Books 2018

ISBN 9789386228970

Typeset in Adobe Caslon Pro by R. Ajith Kumar, New Delhi

Printed at Manipal Technologies Limited

For Mom

1

They took away my shoes. Leather was not allowed inside the old wooden palace with its intricately tiled floors. My loafers would now reside in a cubbyhole by the reception, right under a wooden board that declared: In order to find yourself you have to leave the world behind.

I entered the courtyard with its large pond, its water murky. Pond Water Level said a rickety signboard on one end, Slipping Hazard said another, No Swimming said the third, all in red paint.

A lone turtle was swimming languorously, looking for his mate, unaware that in this man-made pool there perhaps lay only sterility. The turtle dived beneath the mottled lotus leaves, went gliding to the bottom, disappeared. I had come here to do the same.

Unlike on my first visit to Shanthamaaya Sthalam, a

bulging suitcase in hand, packed with books and weather-appropriate garments, all I carried up to my room this time was a small duffel bag.

For the next twenty-eight days, I would wear starched white kurtas and pyjamas. One was already laid out neatly on the bed beside a string of jasmine flowers and jute slippers.

I undressed. The travel-worn, too-snug jeans and the T-shirt that proclaimed 'The Future is Female' joined its fellow inmates inside my bag.

The cotton kurta slid over my arms. Engulfed my head. For a moment I was inside a blinding white tent, transported to my childhood, where the six-inch circumference of a bed sheet around me was large enough to accommodate the vast universe of my imagination.

I pulled on the pyjamas, tugged at the drawstring – not so tight that it chafed against my skin, not so loose that it would fall down around my knees – and made a double knot.

~

The consulting room had not changed in all the years I had been coming here. The sloping tiled roof, the examination bed with its brown cover, the gleaming cream walls that always looked as if they were freshly painted.

The same certificates of accreditation in gilded frames arranged over the copper basin installed into what must have once been an English saab's writing desk and of course Dr Menon, in his cream silk mundu and jubba, an embroidered stole on his shoulder.

The doctor's meticulously groomed moustache and serious demeanour belied the sparkle in his eyes, a remnant of an impish childhood that had held out against the grave endeavour of poring over 5000-year-old Vedic texts.

'My shoulder is better, Dr Menon, but the sleep issues have got worse. I drift off the moment my head touches the pillow, but two hours later my leg jerks me awake. It's as if my brain is giving the body a kick that seems to say, "Wake up!" So I now spend night after night asking myself, "Wake up and do what?" and I still don't have an answer.'

Dr Menon loomed over me as I lay on the examination bed. Eyes closed, he checked my pulse, his fingers hovering over my wrists, my neck, even my navel was not spared, and then in his quiet, unapologetic manner, which usually held a hint of amusement, he declared, 'Anshu, what have you been ingesting? You always come back with a grievous vata imbalance. Chinese food or too much wine again?'

Walking back towards his desk, he continued, 'Parasomnia is what Western medicine calls this disorder, but I am telling you it is because the air element is running through your body helter-skelter. It is vata that is responsible for all your problems. I have told you this right from the first time you came for treatment.'

I first came to Shanthamaaya thirteen years ago with Usha Bua, my favourite aunt and the last link to my father. I could always see bits of him in her, in the rounded shape of her eyebrows, the way she flapped her hands when excited and even in her minuscule earlobes that barely had space to hold an earring, let alone the multiple piercings she sported, tiny diamonds that caught the eye as she moved her head.

I had been in constant pain from two herniated discs in my neck after a nasty fall off a ladder of all things. So when Usha Bua decided to undertake this Ayurvedic pilgrimage for her rheumatoid arthritis, I accompanied her as well. That first trip with its curative, rejuvenating outcome meant that soon a visit to Shanthamaaya became a biennial event.

My memory, though, of the decade-old lecture that Dr Menon was referring to was hazy, but what I did recall clearly was sitting in this room after I had finished my first tenure. I was scheduled to go back home in two days' time and Dr Menon had handed me a printed sheet.

'Please, no non-veg and alcohol for two weeks after this panchakarma treatment.'

4

Thinking of the adjustments I would have to make at home brought another question to my mind. I hesitated at first but then asked, 'Doctor, but what about, you know, physical relations?'

'Anshu, that also entails two weeks of waiting, or all benefits of the treatment are lost.'

'But doctor,' I wailed, 'why didn't you tell me? What if I had not asked you, my whole treatment would have gone down the drain.' To which he replied, 'See the instruction sheet, point no. 6 says, "No vigorous physical activity".'

'That's hardly self-explanatory, Dr Menon. It's not always that vigorous, you know, sometimes you just lie down flat on your back and think of George Clooney!' Dr Menon's expression, his eyebrows reaching high enough to salute his receding hairline, was clearly etched in my memory. Trying to redeem myself, I had ended up falling deeper into the pit with, 'You can also think of patriotic things like your country or the prime minister!'

A horrified pause on both ends, and I squealed, 'No, no, I didn't mean the prime minister, just a slip of the tongue, Dr Menon! Manmohan Singh looming between your legs wouldn't work as a fantasy! I only meant country, like that famous saying "Lie back and think of England". Come to think of it, we as a nation did exactly that for more than a hundred years!'

And I came to an uneasy halt with a nervous giggle.

That evening Dr Menon stopped me near the lotus pond and handed me another printed sheet, this time assigning a new treatment which involved sitting for forty minutes with a funnel made of dough on my head that was slowly filled with hot oil. Below the appointment time, in bold letters it said, 'Shirovasthi: Treatment good for Alzheimer's, Parkinson's and mental imbalances.'

I clambered off the examination bed.

'Yes, yes, of course, I remember, doctor!' I said hastily before he decided to write down another toe-curling treatment for memory loss.

Dr Menon then asked me about my dreams, making a few notations in my file before he thrust a half-filled glass towards me.

This part never got easier. I gagged as the first drop touched my tongue and reluctantly swallowed. It was medicated ghee, mixed with, as I discovered only on my third visit, cow's urine.

The taste was putrid ammonia. The oily decoction slid slowly down inside me, as if a family of slugs was slithering down my throat.

I had once seen a woman who had come from Tokyo for the treatment vomit copiously after her first gulp. She then dragged her husband and left Shanthamaaya immediately, refusing to swallow another drop of the clarified butter that was meant to lubricate the body and soak up all the toxins.

I pinched my nostrils together and tried to throw the rest of the ghee down my throat pretending it was a tequila shot. Failed, retched and then stoically swallowed the rest.

Dr Menon patted my back. 'Well done, Anshu. I don't know why these foreigners make such a fuss about drinking ghee, not so difficult, no?'

Then the hour-long walk began, a straw hat perched on my head, trying to get the oleaginous infusion to settle down, ignoring the belches that were my poor body's desperate attempts to expel it from whichever orifice that would give its kind permission.

I walked circle after circle of the main garden that overlooked the small lake, under jamun trees ripe with fruit. The fallen jamuns crushed under my slippers, which now bore the purple splatters of their sins. My kurta sleeve brushed against jasmine bushes and I stopped, plucked the scented flowers and dropped them into my pocket.

This would be my sole source of perfume here since the Sure deodorant I usually used, by virtue of it being declared a 'chemical weapon' by Dr Menon, was contraband within the hallowed halls of Shanthamaaya.

On my past visits, there had never been more than

twelve or fifteen people in the majestic wooden palace that had been turned into an Ayurvedic hospital. This time there seemed to be fewer. I crossed them along the narrow path, as we all walked in solitary circles, trying to get the ghee to spread within our systems.

A frail-looking young girl with cropped blonde hair, a pair of tubby Russians and two Indian men in their early fifties, the taller one shortening his stride to match the other's pronounced limp.

An hour later, drenched in sweat, I sat by a grove of guava trees. It reminded me of my grandmother's sprawling farm in Panvel. My father lifting me above his shoulders till I managed to pluck some fruit. He would feed them to me, cutting the guava into long slices, sprinkling them with salt and chilli powder. The memory of that tangy sourness filled my mouth and I was tempted to grab one from an overhanging branch but I stopped myself.

In Shanthamaaya you could only eat when the big bell heralded mealtimes and have just the simple fare that was placed on the brass plates. A strict regime, one that was difficult to adhere to. No wonder my sister always refused to come.

Mandira, two years older than me and her voice two notches higher than mine, but close enough for us to pull pranks on our extended family, had called while I was driving here, starting off abruptly as always. 'Mummy just told me you are going to that Kerala place again for the hundredth time! Did she call you?'

I replied, 'Yes, Mandy, she called me, but it was mainly to complain about Manisha Tai and how fed–'

Mandira usually had a reason for calling and there was very little anyone could do to derail her. You could yank at the chain incessantly but this hurtling train would only stop at its destined station.

She cut me short saying, 'But what I still can't understand is what do they charge so much for in that hellhole? You keep saying there isn't even a TV in the room, no swimming pool, and not even bloody room service!'

Mandira would have just returned from her regular ladies' lunch. I could see her, sitting upright on her grey couch, a cigarette in her hand, overdressed in her stifling, overdecorated flat in Punjabi Bagh.

I took a swig of water from the plastic bottle in my bag and then a deep breath to control my irritation, as she went on, 'Mummy was saying, "If Anshu only took half that money and spent it at Dr Chandra's, then she would also be tip-top like you!"'

'Mandy, I don't know why Mummy and you keep talking about me constantly! I never discuss you with her!'

A guilty pause. Then my sister tried to mollify me.

'We just worry about you, that's all. Listen to me, Anshu, forget all this holistic hocus-pocus. What you need is to just get some Botox done! If you fill in the cracks in the plaster and give the building a fresh coat of paint you find it easier to get tenants. It's the same with us women, you know!'

Barbed retorts flew from my mind and banged against the wall of my gritted teeth. I took another deep breath and reminded myself that while blood is thicker than water, it has a tendency to congeal unpleasantly.

'Mandy, everyone is not desperately trying to hold on to their crumbling youth. I'm fine the way I am.'

And to blunt the sharp edge of my tongue before it ripped into my sister further, I said, 'You do get more comfortable in your skin as you get older but that is probably because the poor thing is also not as tight as it once used to be. So you are partially right there.'

My sister laughed, a short, guttural bark, and I added, 'Come here with me at least once, Mandy, you will feel a big shift.'

'Anshu, I swear I would rather go off to Tihar jail!'

But as usual she didn't know when to stop. 'I'm just concerned, that's all. All you seem to be doing these last few years is working obsessively or taking these odd trips to your beloved santhalam, shantalam, I can't even pronounce it! Mummy says that you hardly go out and she has to remind you to even thread your upper lip, for God's sake.'

I could imagine their hour-long conversations, a washing line tied at one end in Bombay and the other in Delhi with me left to hang and dry in the middle.

'Mandy, I am fine, you and Mummy have just made it a point to find faults in me. I am sick of this "poor Anshu" business. So what if I have been focusing on the school? You think businesses just run by themselves? Before giving me lectures ask yourself what you have done in the last few years aside from depleting your bank account and inflating your dermatologist's? Stop getting on my case.' Only sisters can hurl nuclear weapons at each other and come out unscathed.

Our conversation was mercifully cut short because Malini, the senior teacher at my preschool, was on call waiting and, as I soon discovered, rather anxious. An abnormally strong preschooler-cum-sociopath had tried to strangle his classmate with the strap of her Chhota Bheem water bottle within a day of my being away.

Mandira would never understand why I liked coming to Shanthamaaya. She didn't like regimentation, while I revelled in the fact that I did not have to think about what to wear, when to eat or even what to eat. The freedom of a mind unchained from the mundane worries of should I put on a peach lipstick or do a matte beige, should I make butter chicken or should I grab a sandwich. At Shanthamaaya, all the shoulds were replaced with musts, as if we were part of a cult, Scientology, Children of God, the Manson Family. This freedom from our own urges, safely cocooned in rules.

~

The young girl stopped near the guava trees and hesitated before sitting at the far end of the bench.

'Jenna,' she said, her voice grave and surprisingly deep for one so slight of build. She had a gentle smile, quivering at the edges, unsure if it should be wider. The long bangs hanging down her slender face lent it a pleasing softness.

'I'm Anshu,' I said. 'First time here?'

'Yes, I just came in this morning and this place, it's a little disorienting.'

She held her head precisely, straight, her chin tucked in, the muscles at the back of her neck elongated as if she was balancing a pile of invisible bricks on her head.

'I have done this a few times, Jenna, and fair warning, within five days you will be more than willing to do a dramatic, over-the-wall jailbreak and run for your life!

But stick around and it does get better or perhaps like all prisoners, some of their own circumstances, you just get used to the misery.'

I leaned back against the wooden bench, peering at her and unable to discern any obvious ailments. 'So tell me what brings a nice girl like you to what my sister kindly calls Dante's first circle of hell?'

A small sound that could be mistaken for a laugh escaped her and she said, 'Psoriasis.' She pulled her sleeve up, letting me see the angry red scabs all over her elbow.

'And you?'

'I have some ancient broken parts, all clumsily put together. Everything works but only now you can hear the joints grinding and squeaking.' I rotated my shoulders and the creaking sound was impressive even to my ears. 'A nifty party trick!' an orthopaedic surgeon with a Donald Duck tie had told me many years ago. 'But this time it's primarily to sort out my sleep issues!'

She touched her thin hair, her scalp peeping through in places. 'You have such nice hair, most Indians do, I have noticed,' she said, her hand moving with delicate grace as she pointed towards my long, dark hair that I had oiled and plaited.

I shrugged. 'My one pride and joy! I guess all that coconut oil really turned out to be as effective as the advertisements on television used to claim, after all. Growing up, my mother would upend bottles of oil on our heads like she was about to fry French fries on our scalps.'

For all her self-effacing manner, Jenna was a trained gymnast – 'A performance artist,' she said. And like me she was also here for the twenty-eight-day programme; three weeks being the minimum that Shanthamaaya deigns to open its gates for inmates to balance our out-of-whack bodies.

According to the tenets of Ayurveda, we are made up of three biological energies. Doshas they call it. Vata, pitta and kapha. These doshas are based on proportions of air, ether, fire, earth and water in individuals, elements that govern the physical processes. Every individual is defined by his or her dominating dosha, every illness by an imbalance in the doshas.

Jenna seemed the quintessential airy vata, delicately boned with a quick mind that scampered like a sparrow. In her body, it was pitta, the fire element, responsible for all metabolic functions that was out of balance and waging war on her skin.

We were opposites as far as Ayurveda was concerned. I was ruled by pitta, fiery-tempered and mercurial. Though a novice would perhaps have categorized me as a kapha with my generously sized eyes, masses of hair and the broad shoulders that would suit me well if part-time wrestling were to ever become a hobby. I also had what my mother graciously called my 'oversized lips and hips!' as if they were bags that I would have to pay extra for to check in at airline counters. All these traits normally denoted the water–earth element, though I wish I had their temperament instead, their slow, calm minds.

The bell rang for lunch and we walked towards the covered porch, sitting next to each other on the hard benches facing the sprawling gardens. I picked at my roti and bland dal, leaving the boiled spinach alone, while Jenna was unable to swallow a single bite.

The next few days passed as if I were a cuckoo in a grand old clock. At regular intervals, the clock would chime regimentally and I would pop out of my room which overlooked the dining room.

The shrill wake-up call before dawn, water hastily splashed on to my face, scrambling to reach the yoga class for sun salutations, where the teacher's instructions mingled with prayers from an unseen temple that drifted into the wooden pavilion along with the morning light.

An hour later, we would once again hear the clanging of the brass bell and, salivating like Pavlov's dogs, we would walk to the porch to often be greeted with nothing more than a solitary fruit. All the patients were instructed to reach the clinic by mid-morning where we had to swallow increasing amounts of ghee before walking around the yard, diligently finishing the fourteen circles the doctors had ordered.

Sometimes I would spot young children from the nearby village climbing over the wall in worn shirts and dingy vests peeking at us. I would wave out at them, pause for a moment, pull out my Nikon from the sling bag and take a few pictures.

A pigtailed little girl with bottle-green bangles, two little boys with large eyes reminiscent of Margaret Keane's paintings. I wondered what went through the children's minds when they saw us, people in white, walking endlessly, round and round the garden. Did they think this was an asylum? And we the deranged inmates in need of electric shocks?

Coming together for three meals a day meant we got to know each other soon enough. Jenna, her spirit as frail as her slight frame, loudly signalling: fragile – handle with care. The Russians, Vyacheslav and Afanasy, were here to lose weight. The other two men were from Bangalore, a couple it seemed. Javed who with his long face and aquiline nose reminded me of Nehru, especially with the small flowers he liked to tuck into his kurta buttonhole, while the only touch of ostentation on his partner, Anil, was a serpentine ring.

2

On the fourth day, just before noon, voices drifted up through my bedroom window. It was an unusual occurrence within the monotonous regularity of Shanthamaaya. No one was permitted into the dining room till the bell tolled at lunchtime.

I shut my book and, curious, leaned out from the wooden window, pushing the heavy green shutters as far as they would go, peering through the gaps in the red tiled roof of the dining porch.

I saw the mundu-clad server carrying a tray of refreshments and two people facing the lush gardens. I could only see parts of a shoulder and two backs, but the white cotton marked them as patients, new arrivals probably, who were being given the customary banana and cinnamon bark water with honey. A moment later, the man turned to look at his companion.

I fell back on the hard mattress with a thud. The nineteenth-century bed, which groaned each time I tossed and turned at night, let out a creak as loud as a gunshot. My hands were trembling, and I felt more nauseous than I did in the few seconds after swallowing the ghee each morning.

There sitting on that porch, that light-eyed man, the one with salt-and-pepper hair and a decisive mind, a pitta like me, was my ex-husband and that woman whom I could not quite see and whose inner element I was unaware of, unless bitch is accepted as an undiscovered fourth dosha in Ayurveda, was his young wife.

I sat numb, as voices drifted through the window, invading my room, coiling around me. I wanted to take my small bag, run down the wooden steps to the porch, catch a taxi, say 'vegam' (the only word I knew in Malayalam), urging the driver to go faster and faster, the destination irrelevant as long as I put enough kilometres between here and there.

A few minutes later I crossed my legs, inhaled and began a series of breathing exercises. Kapalbhati, bhastrika, anuloma viloma, holding, and then letting go. Cycles that I have mastered and done so many times that if they had wheels I would have reached Ladakh by now.

But the cycles led me to an even more remote place, a calm place inside my head. I opened my eyes and asked myself why I had to be the one to run away. In the victory of her thighs over mine should I give this up to her as well?

The temperamental shower within the spotless bathroom needed skilful coaxing, adjusting the right faucet and its dribbles of cold water and turning the left faucet to precisely 35 degrees so that scalding hot water did not come gushing out. I stood under the cascade of water, washing my hair with the foul-smelling herbal soap in the bathroom.

I had to stay on at Shanthamaaya for a practical reason as well. While the folks here were very generous with their noxious ghee, I doubted if their kindness would stretch as far as giving me a refund. Shanthamaaya was an expensive indulgence, one that I carefully planned for and looked forward to. I dried my hair with a thin, striped cloth that masqueraded as a towel and decided that I was going to stick around and to hell with them.

They were gone by the time I came out of the bathroom, the dining room deserted. When the bell rang for lunch, I walked down the stairs, reassuring myself that, having just had their refreshments, they would probably spend the afternoon resting in their room.

I entered the empty dining room and sat at my usual spot, the fourth table from the entrance. The Russians soon arrived and a few minutes later Jenna, looking pale and wrung out, walked in and sat down beside me.

'I have been throwing up since the morning,' she said. 'Dr Pillai says it's normal but I can't do this any more, I just want to give up.'

Jenna had lost a startling amount of weight in the last few days. Vatas tend to be slender and she had been unable to eat more than a few morsels.

Dr Pillai who was looking after her, a pretentious man with tiny, beady eyes, was not one of my favourites. 'I will talk to Dr Menon,' I said eventually. 'You liked the porridge, right? Maybe they can give you some every day. Give me a list of what you are able to keep down and let's see if we can ask them to alter your diet.'

I wanted to finish my ragi roti and sprouts as soon as possible and go back to my room and when she asked me if I would talk to the doctor that very day, I nodded, chewing the last bite furiously.

I saw him as I was finishing up, taking a last sip of water from the brass tumbler. He was standing at the porch entrance.

For a brief moment I could sense the surge of adrenaline, the fight or flee instinct in the quick darting of his eyes, and then it was gone. An affable ease, like a well-crafted garment that he slipped into, as I had seen him do numerous times, slid into place.

Shalini was standing just behind him. I recognized her from pictures I had pored over obsessively all those years ago, stalking various Facebook accounts night after night – masochist behaviour, like rubbing chilli powder into my eyes.

He walked towards me as if he was pleased to see an old friend and said, 'Anshu, what are you doing here?' In spite of the churning in my stomach, I managed to appear nonchalant. 'What does anyone do here, Jay, drink ghee, vomit and hope.'

I stood up and headed to the sink in the far corner to wash my hands, flustered but holding on to my precarious self-possession.

As I went past Shalini, I tapped her, unthinkingly with my right hand, the one with the dal-and-sprout-coated fingers, leaving a turmeric stain on her shoulder. I said, 'You must be Shalini, welcome to Shanthamaaya, I hope you like it here.'

~

The day passed in tedious treatments. First, an ancient steam bath where I squatted inside a wooden cupboard with a cut-out for my head, the steam being delivered through pipes attached to boiling kettles on the adjacent gas range.

Then an hour of green poultices placed on my frozen

shoulder, followed by a massage of noxious medicated sesame oil and an unexpected beauty treatment. The short attendant, Deepti, her smile matching the warmth that her name implied, said, 'Doctor told red rice and milk pack for the face,' and at my protests she gently pushed me back on the wooden pallet. 'You try and see, skin will shine like anything.'

Kneaded, scrubbed and washed clean, I returned to my room exhausted. When the bell rang for dinner, the thought of the bland meal or perhaps the equally unappetizing prospect of seeing the happy couple made me skip my meal.

The open window, like an old wireless, sent me creaky bulletins of the scene below me – the clattering of plates, murmuring of voices and then a dull silence broken only by the low-pitched hum of insects from the distant bushes somewhere in the dark.

My eyes were weary from poring over a musty book from the Shanthamaaya library. I switched the light off and decided to try to sleep.

Lying in the shadowy room, my head on the pillow, the bed creaking with the slightest shift, I began my counting ritual: one, two, three. Numbers failed me that night and I tried another way of inviting sleep, by singing the alphabet song in my head like a toddler learning her letters.

A knock startled me as I reached 'QRST' and I put

on the night lamp. Jenna must have come to check on me, worried if I was sick, just as I had gone knocking on her door yesterday.

I unlocked the heavy wooden door and, rubbing my eyes with one hand, pulled it open. In the small pool of light from the overhead lamp stood my ex-husband, shifting from one foot to the other, his kurta moving with him like he was waving a white flag of truce between us.

The first time I had seen Jay was also on the other side of a wooden door, my friend Prashant's door to be precise. It was a lazy Sunday and, seeking refuge in my childhood friend's house, I had not thought twice about answering the doorbell when Prashant was in the bathroom, answering nature's call and ploughing through a pile of comic books.

Opening the door, I saw an athletically built man standing on the threshold, the short sleeves of his black T-shirt rolled high up on his arms.

His angular face had a challenging harmony, both sides aligned in perfect symmetry, and he had startlingly grey eyes. I kept gazing at him, at this beautiful-looking man. In a country where the male species tended to be more peahen than peacock, he was all glorious, preening plumage.

The first words he said to me were 'nice face' and when

I turned away from the door to call out to Prashant he added, 'Bad backside.' And I was hooked.

Carrot and stick, wonderful and not good enough.

I would spend years sifting through the vinegar, looking for the bits of honey, with him throwing in both the ingredients according to his whimsy. It was a pattern unconsciously crafted to keep me twirling to please. But all that came later.

That day, in the twelve steps from Prashant Sunder's main door to his bathroom, I began falling in love with the man walking behind me, while his gaze probably stayed fixed to my backside. A bum that in reality had not been bad at all.

In fact he would later say that he had been immediately attracted by its roundness. 'Your ass, my love, is big and wonderful. You know, if you lose a few pounds you can easily be one of those Baywatch girls in the red swimsuits, you are all curves and no straight lines.'

He claimed he had used the 'bad' just like a boy punches a girl in fourth grade to show her that he likes her. Slice and lick, kick and kiss. So he jabbed at my ego, and along with my bottom he ended up with my heart in his hands as well.

But today Jay was not here to talk about my bum or what a bum he had in fact turned out to be in the end.

'Jay, what are you doing here?'

With a wry smile he tossed back the words I had used that afternoon: 'What does anyone do here, Anshu, drink ghee, vomit and hope.'

'Very funny, Jay, but next time, come up with your own wisecracks.'

He leaned against the door and said, 'Imitation is the best form of flattery.'

'It's "imitation is the sincerest form of flattery", Jay, and since that is Oscar Wilde you still have not come up with a single original thought.'

He laughed. 'What to do, Anshu, I am a plagiarist.'

And before I could stop myself, I said, 'And here I thought you were only a philanderer.'

He drew back, a frown adding to the fine network of lines on his forehead, and my hand instinctively moved before I realized that it was not my job any more to smoothen out the creases, not from his forehead and not from his shirts. He was ageing well, I thought – at fifty-two, he still retained a youthful quality, sturdy, agile.

'I didn't come here to get drawn into old arguments, Anshu. You can say what you like but I will not sink to your level.'

I had not seen Jay for seven years but it had not taken me five minutes with him to once again be on the back foot. Irritated, I mumbled, 'It's just a joke, for God's sake, you don't have to go into some Gautam Buddha mode!'

He shook his head. 'Look, Anshu, I know this is awkward for you and I swear I had no idea you were going to be here. When you didn't come for dinner I understood how uncomfortable you must be. The time we came here together, I don't remember you ever missing a meal. Well, no one does with the tiny amounts they give us anyway.'

'We came together just once, Jay, and maybe I didn't miss any meals on that trip, perhaps the other times I did, how do you know? Stop making assumptions.'

He put his hands up ruefully. 'Yes, yes, whatever you say, you miss meals all the time here and live on ghee and fresh air! I just wanted to tell you that if you want to leave, I totally understand and, you know what, I will book it for you, any time you want to come, next month, maybe? Consider it a birthday present from me in advance.'

I interrupted this grand display of him playing the big man to my weak little woman. 'Why should I go? I was here before you and I am the one who introduced you to this bloody place in the first place. If you care so much about my discomfort, let me book a taxi for you and you leave.'

'Despite what you believe, Anshu, I care, and I thought this way it would be easier.'

I looked at the small scar on his right cheek. His mother had said he had fallen from their second-floor balcony and survived. A tree had broken his fall and he had escaped unscathed only to cut his cheek on the sharp edge of a pebble on the ground.

I shook my head firmly. 'I am not leaving, Jay.' And then, though I regretted it the moment it came out, I blurted, 'So you married her eventually? You could have sent a card at least.'

'Would you have come?'

'Who knows, maybe,' I said. 'By the way where is she, your wife, now?'

'She is in the room,' he answered shortly.

'And where does she think you are?'

'How does it matter to you, Anshu?'

'Tell me, I am curious. You couldn't have told her you are going for a drive here, "To get cigarettes and to clear my head," like you started telling me right at the very end?'

'You know me in and out, don't you, Anshu?' He burst out laughing. 'I told her I was going for a walk and, yes, to clear my head.'

A chuckle escaped me, though I didn't know what I was laughing at, myself or the irony of fate.

He tilted his head away from the light, now more shadow than skin, the laugh still resonating between us like the sound from a conch shell at the beginning of Diwali pujas, altering the vibrations in the atmosphere.

Leaning forward, his hand on the door, Jay said, 'You are looking well, Anshu. Shanthamaaya always did that for you, I remember. All right, stay then, but let's just make this easy for each other, shall we?'

'Yes, Jay, I promise not to bribe them to give you extra enemas.' A glib remark that achieved its objective, bringing half a smile to his face. I moved his hand and shut the door.

3

An old lady in a blue sari. A plate of barfi with two flies. I am throwing green chillies at an unseen adversary, my arm banging against the headboard, mimicking the action.

I held each tiny dream by its tail, hoping to climb on to the spine of the gossamer beast and fall into deep slumber on its back. My grip loosened and tightened, I slept and woke. And I was almost relieved when the alarm rang.

I washed my face, got into a fresh pair of gleaming cotton pyjamas and headed for the yoga class.

All the patients of Shanthamaaya were gathered on the stairs leading to the pavilion, waiting for the teacher to arrive. Jenna, yawning, her boyish chest expanding with the effort, braless as usual, her nipples a dark shadow beneath her white kurta. Javed and Anil, leaning against the railing next to the Russians. Afanasy's florid complexion scorched a flaming red by the Kerala sun.

Jay, his kurta sleeves rolled up to his elbows, stood at a distance under the mango tree, next to a disgruntled-looking Shalini. Her voice travelled over in fragments to where we were standing.

'I hate this place ... go to a spa in Thailand ... horrible ghee ... why should I ... all these ill people ... nothing wrong with me ... want to go back today.'

I couldn't hear what Jay was saying. His voice was pitched low and soft.

Eventually he walked over and greeted everyone with a cheery 'good morning' and asked me if I had slept well with a smile that brought out the dimple in his right cheek. Shalini ambled over to the group, greeting us with a cursory nod as if this was all the effort she could make for us. Kesava, the senior yoga teacher, came along moments later.

I pulled out a yoga mat, a purple one today, off the stacked pile near the entrance and took my place. We were meant to make two parallel lines on either side of the teacher and I went to my favourite spot facing the big window.

On certain mornings, the glass pane seemed like a cinema screen that started off dark before dawn and then slowly began its sunlight-aided projection of tall trees, swaying branches and the lake.

Carrying two yoga mats, Jay began laying them down side by side in the row ahead. He had always done the same for me when we had come together.

A wince, even after all this time. A hastening of my heartbeat. I was more than capable of carrying my own mat, but it pricked, like an ant bite, a small burn that soon began itching incessantly.

She had him to carry her burdens, rolled-up rubbery ones and myriad others, and I had no one. I changed places with Jenna and moved to the front of the class, claiming I didn't want to practise under the fan.

A green apple for breakfast. A glass of water infused with fennel meant to quell the excess air running through my joints. Downing ghee. Combating nausea. Then headphones plugged in, a hat on my head and the fourteen circles around the garden.

The happy couple were also ambling along, like everyone else, on the same circular route as me. Stuck in my fixed orbit, I hurried on, round and round, trying to dodge the occasional meteors of her smug smiles and his hand brushing against her waist.

~

'Turn over, Anshu madam,' Deepti said, and I flipped on to my back on the huge wooden table shaped like a boat.

After sheepishly asking Dr Menon if he had something in his repertoire to vanquish cellulite, I had been assigned an hour-long session of udwarthanam, a turmeric powder massage.

My skin was burning from the friction generated by Deepti's hands rubbing my hips when I felt a rumbling in my stomach like the harbinger of doom. Halfway through the massage, I began throwing up, though there was nothing in my stomach but fetid, sour bile and ghee.

I trekked to my room, vomited four more times and with black spots crossing my vision and a spinning head, feeling and probably looking like the possessed girl in *The Exorcist*, I sent for Dr Menon.

'This has never happened before, doctor,' I muttered and Dr Menon, holding my wrist in his hand, listening to a litany of my sins that the beating pulse seemed to whisper only to him, said, 'Normally it takes you seven days to reach saturation, but this time it is almost full already, that is why you are throwing up.'

He continued, 'If a room is dirty and if you fill it with people and more people till there is no place to add even one more person and then you start pushing all these people out, let me tell you, once they leave the room, you will find it is clean.'

There was an expression of reverence on Dr Menon's face as he expounded further on his favourite subject. 'Their hands, feet and even their noses touching the wall will have wiped the walls as they are pushed outside. It is the same with ghee. We fill your body with so much ghee till there is no room for even one drop more. We then purge you and, with the ghee, all the fat-soluble toxins stuck in your organs, in your liver, kidney, all get pushed out as well.'

'Doctor, do you have any treatment for amnesia?'

Dr Menon frowned. 'Of course, in Ayurveda we have treatments for everything! Let me tell you, Western science has not even learned the things that we have forgotten. Tell me, who needs this amnesia treatment?'

I laughed feebly. 'You do, doctor! For letting them book Jay here at the same time as me and for telling me this ghee story that I have heard half a dozen times already.' Then I turned my head and threw up in the blue plastic bucket once again.

That evening, I had recovered enough to participate in a Shanthamaaya ritual that believed in keeping the patients hungry and the animals satiated. Walking down the narrow brick-flanked path and over the mossy stone steps to the fish pond, I could see my fellow inmates huddled together, listening to Kesava, who was giving a familiar discourse.

'Your life is like a bank account. You deposit with good karma and you withdraw with bad karma. At the end it gets totalled. If you have a big balance of good karma left, you will go to a better life. If your bank account is going into minus, then you may even be reborn as any small thing, like a mosquito, or an ant, in your next life. Feeding animals is just one of the ways to earn good karma. Come, take the bread, break it into small pieces and feed it to the fish.'

A fresh contingent of people had arrived at Shanthamaaya that afternoon. The receptionist, Surya, had told me that they were now running at full capacity, but it was still a surprise to suddenly encounter new inmates in the spa.

Jay grabbed a loaf from Kesava and passed it to a shorter man. As I drew closer, I realized it was Lalit Makhija, Jay's cousin. My ex-husband seemed in unusually high spirits, and Lalit seemed to start each time Jay threw his arm over his shoulder or clapped him on the back in a grand show of bonhomie.

Looking at Jay's exuberant smiles, I began wondering if my ex-husband was here to balance his dosha and to feed the fish or if this was one of his schemes, as I had seen over the years, to try to land the big whale.

Jay must have already told Lalit that I was in Shanthamaaya because he didn't look surprised to see me. He smiled, a wide, gummy smile, and pulled me towards him for an unrequired hug, saying, 'Anshu, you haven't changed at all, still look like Bipasha Basu's younger sister!'

This was something he had said each time we bumped into each other, though the only thing I had in common with that sex siren was our dusky skin tones.

Uncle Octopus is how my sister referred to Lalit after meeting him at a few family gatherings. His proclivity towards running his hands liberally over all the ladies during greetings and group photographs was rather well known.

'Jay finally convinced me to come here. He guarantees that they will fix me up!'

Jay laughed ingratiatingly.

'Lalit, you don't need anybody to fix you up if even half of what I hear about your post-divorce escapades is true.'

There was a weary-looking young man standing next to Lalit. 'And have you met this chap? I had to share the car from the airport here with him, Vivaan Dalvi,' Lalit said. 'You have heard of the company Sundara, na, oils, soap and cream, all the things you women get conned into buying, all his.'

He turned to Vivaan. 'Your work crisis must involve people coming up to you and saying, "We were trying to make the moisturizer smell like jasmine but big tragedy, sirji, it is now smelling of roses!'

Vivaan shrugged with an affable smile that belied the dark circles under his sunken eyes. He was lean, with the quintessential beard that millennials seem to sport these days, and a lot taller than my ex-husband, who was now vigorously shaking his hand in the manner of a politician canvassing for votes.

'Yes, Lalit, I am nothing more than a snake oil salesman!'

'See, Vivaan thinks he is a punny, funny guy!' said Lalit cackling like he was the host of *Comedy Nights with Kapil* and we the cross-dressing sidekicks.

Leaving Shalini aiming her finest simpering smiles at Lalit, I walked towards the group of newcomers.

Names were thrown, so swiftly that I struggled to catch them all. An older woman, Madhu Rao, with immaculate red lipstick, who was accompanied by Babaji, her personal-guru-cum-soothsayer.

Pam, a travel blogger, deeply tanned and all the way from London, who I had seen at lunch as well, taking pictures of a crumbling statue adjacent to the pond, calling out to her companion, 'Glenda darling, have a look at this, it's terribly charming!'

They had set up two large tables in the front garden for dinner. Lanterns hung from tree boughs, wind chimes tinkled from others. There were dinner napkins, rolled and tied with jute rope and white flowers, place cards with our first names written in blue ink.

I walked around the table, looking for my seat, and discovered that I had been placed opposite Lalit, with Jay seated between Shalini and me.

Age had taught me that life was often about finding the simplest way to solve even the most complicated problems. I found one. My place card clenched in my hand, I surreptitiously switched it with Anil's, so I was seated next to Jenna, at the other table.

Gleaming brass plates with little bowls of beans mixed with grated coconut and boiled okra were placed before us. Pam, sitting opposite me, was asking questions, one after another, as if she was conducting a rapid-fire quiz.

She and Glenda were touring India, reviewing holistic centres for their travel blog. They had already been to the Wildflower Spa in Shimla and Ananda in the Himalayas.

'You can drink beer and even Coke there, what do you get here?'

'Ghee and only ghee,' I said, 'as you will discover tomorrow.'

As we finished our dinner, Anil walked over to our table and began complaining to Javed.

'I am going to tell them at the reception that I want to sit with you for meals and not to shuffle us around.'

'I didn't know you would miss me so quickly,' Javed laughed. 'Very heartening after all these years.'

'Stop being sarcastic! I am already in a bad mood as it is. That woman,' Anil said pointing in Shalini's direction, 'she is very irritating.'

Apparently Shalini had asked Anil if Javed and he were a couple. 'When I said yes, she asked me, "So which one of you is the girl?" Is this anything to ask? So stupid!'

'So what did you say?'

'What is there to say, Javed, that yes I have a secret vagina! I said that it's a silly question and then she says, "No, I meant are you a top or a bottom?" How can you ask someone these things when you barely know them? Her husband tried to change the topic but she just went on and on. Javed, don't you dare leave me alone with those people again.'

I looked over at their table. Jay was standing by the table trying to talk to Lalit while his child-bride was tugging at his arm repeatedly.

4

The Prince Restaurant and Bar had eight aluminium tables, rickety chairs and the best South Indian coffee, or so I had been told by Shanthamaaya residents over the years. Coffee addicts may travel halfway across the planet for a cure but often just cannot give up their daily dose.

A fifteen-minute walk from Shanthamaaya's sanctified gates, the Prince was also the only place that offered, along with cheap beer and fried prawns, the possibility of your phone connecting with the world at large.

It was not uncommon to see us 'ghosts', as I called my white-clad fellow members of the dysfunctional dosha club, walking up and down that stretch of the road or sitting around the Prince's dented tables, ordering bottles of water as our admittance fee.

Every afternoon, just after lunch, when the sun was

blazing and sensible animals were scurrying for shade, I would put on a straw hat and walk to the Prince.

I would dutifully switch on my phone and within minutes, as if she had wrapped her umbilical cord around my phone and was waiting for an electric tug, Mummy would call.

Today she began with, 'Anshu, your Instagram now says, "Brilliant at daydreaming-lousy at cooking!"'

'Yes, I know, Mummy!'

'Tell me something, beta, if I have a little paunch should I wear a bikini or cover it up in a one-piece?'

'I guess, wear the swimsuit?' I replied, wondering why my mother had suddenly started asking me for tips on bathing suits.

She said, 'Yes! That is exactly what I am saying. Why tell people you can't cook? Just like with a big stomach, cover up your defects, Anshu! There is no need to reveal everything to everyone.'

Some families put out advertisements in newspapers, some distribute pictures. My mother, I suspected, had lately been using my Instagram page to showcase my attributes to prospective mothers-in-law at Khar Gymkhana, who were presumably looking for suitable wives for their long in the tooth, deranged or divorced sons.

As my mother prattled on, I was surprised to spot Pam and Glenda peering at their phones under the Prince's tattered awning. Vivaan was also sitting at another table in the corner. Exchanging pleasantries after the yoga class this morning, I had found him amiable enough, so when he raised a cup of coffee as a silent greeting and waved me over, I bid Mummy a hasty goodbye and walked towards him.

'You have already discovered this secret gem, Vivaan! It took me two trips before I even knew we could leave the gates!' I said and sat down across him, ordering myself a bottle of room temperature Bisleri water.

Vivaan had a steady gaze, the kind of eyes that you wanted to glance away from because they seemed to see more than you wanted to divulge. He looked at me rather sheepishly and said, 'I wish I could take the credit, but Jay told all of us about it this morning.' Indicating his cup of coffee, he asked, 'You won't have some?' as the aroma wafted towards me.

I shook my head. 'I don't here. At home I drink four cups of black coffee a day,' I said, 'only gave it up when—' and I abruptly stopped.

A silence that was about to turn awkward was broken when Pam pulled out a half-empty bottle of Pinot Grigio from her white satchel and topped up two glasses with the white wine. Her voice was already slurring as she loudly proclaimed, 'This is the real detox for the soul!' and then immediately began complaining to her friend about the price of avocados at Tesco.

I turned to Vivaan and said in low tones, 'If I had to guess her dosha, I would say Pam is a vata. Impulsive, a love for excitement and' – I looked at her brittle hair and chapped skin – 'a dry constitution. I hope she doesn't have another typical vata characteristic.'

When Vivaan looked inquiringly at me, I whispered, 'Chronic constipation, most can count themselves lucky if they can pass little hard pellets every alternate day!'

A companionable smile again, his eyes still cautiously reflective as he leisurely sipped his coffee and said, 'And me? What do you think I am?'

I examined him carefully, taking in the balanced bone structure, short, square fingers. 'I will try but in order to be really accurate I have to ask you some questions.'

He nodded slowly and I noted the tentativeness.

I was certain that Dr Pillai, who he had been assigned to, must have already told him his primary dosha and that made it all the more challenging for me.

And so it began.

'Do you remember things easily and then forget?'

He paused. 'No, it takes me time to absorb things, but once I do it stays in my mind like it's been stuck with Fevicol.'

'What kind of dreams do you have?'

'I don't dream.'

'Everyone dreams!'

'Then let's say that I don't remember my dreams.'

'Do you think in words, pictures or feelings?'

'I don't know what that means, Anshu.'

I elaborated, 'If I ask you to look back at what you were doing last summer, do you remember it in words, like lazy, busy, warm; or pictures, sitting on a plane, lying on the beach; or emotions, happiness, boredom?'

He closed his eyes, silent for a moment, and said, 'Pictures. I went sailing in Greece, I can see the blue ocean, no, wait, it's almost green in places.'

'All right,' I said, delighting in this little game. 'Next, do you like change?'

'Not particularly!'

'Show me your tongue.'

He laughed. 'I don't think even Dr Pillai examined me so thoroughly.' But he stuck his tongue out sportingly.

'Well, thank you, you can put the tongue back in now. And the last question – what ails you, why are you here, Vivaan?'

'Osteosarcoma, cancer of the tibia.'

A sinking in my stomach, like we had been on a meandering road trip, singing along with the radio when our car had slammed into a desultory animal.

I said all the things people say in these circumstances.

A jumble of meaningless words to fill the chasm that had suddenly opened up between us.

He waited for me to finish and then in his measured voice he said, 'We all have to go at some point, but we walk around pretending we are going to live forever, don't we? I just have what I like to call a sneak-peek at my mortality, bas, that's all.'

That level gaze again and then with a deliberate levity he leaned back into his chair and said, 'Achha, you have got all your answers, now tell me, what am I?'

'You are a remarkable man' were the words waiting to take flight. Instead I placed my straw hat jauntily on his head and tried to borrow some of his ease. 'The sorting hat from Harry Potter would probably proclaim "Gryffindor" but mine from the equally hallowed halls of Shanthamaaya's gift shop says dual dosha, kapha–pitta.'

We continued sitting together. In between checking my emails, I tried amusing Vivaan with anecdotes of my previous trips here. An old, ingrained habit, hiding behind banal chatter, because I have found that often silence, like the back of a gleaming spoon, unexpectedly turns into a mirror.

I finished the bottle of water and we were about to head back to Shanthamaaya when I saw the man that my sister had spent the past few years abusing walking towards us, a cigarette in his hand.

Back in the day, I used to often laugh and tell our friends, 'Jay can live without me but not without his Marlboros.' Little did I know then that a joke is only amusing because it has a kernel of truth in it.

He was striding along the dusty pathway, his sleeves rolled up as usual, and I found myself staring at him. Like I used to in the days when we were together, when I would see him from afar, across a crowded room, in the next aisle at the supermarket, from my window playing volleyball below in the building garden.

~

A swirling fan, a minuscule hole in the mosquito net, a crack in the ceiling. I lay motionless in bed. Two hours of sleep, a jerk in my left leg and I was wide awake now. Sometimes I found it hard to reconcile the person I was in the day with this sleepless wreck. How can something feel whole in the sun and disintegrate by moonlight?

My mind drifted to my sister. Mandira always said that she knew me inside out, like I was a skirt she inverted at will and periodically examined the hem.

When I told her that Jay was here, she had urged me to leave Shanthamaaya.

'Why do you want this unnecessary complication?'

'I have already paid, Mandira, should I just waste it?'

'That main doctor is your great pal, you told me yourself! I am sure if you explain the situation, he will get you your goddamn refund, Anshu.'

'And then what? Let Jay and that scrawny slut think that they affect me so much that I had to run away? Please, I would rather die! I will be fine, they don't bother me at all.'

'I know what you are like inside, Anshu, though you put up this big brave act. I remember what a mess you were when he left!'

A mess. I had blotted out that mess along with the woman who used to ensure that a steaming cup of coffee, with exactly a teaspoon of milk and half a teaspoon of sugar, was ready on the bedside table before her husband opened his eyes, the one who cried on her sister's shoulder and into countless glasses of wine for months. That woman was long gone.

After the divorce, I had taken all the photographs of our holidays and deleted all the ones that we had taken together. It was an alternative to cropping his head out of the frame and replacing it with a big, round, generic smiley because that was the extent of my Photoshop abilities.

The photographs that I had kept, I barely looked at any more. Pictures of me giggling under the shade of my white hat, in front of the Palazzo Vecchio, a dab of raspberry gelato on my chin that I am about to wipe off with the cuff of my new shirt. Laughing, my Nikon in my hand, my head against a train window, crumbs of crisps littering the seats, endless cactus fields bordering the track, from Salta to the Chilean border.

I couldn't think about the most joyful moments of my life without seeing him sitting across me, sharing them. I had managed to crop him out of photographs but not out of my memories.

I had explained to Mandira repeatedly that my stubbornness in staying here had nothing to do with Jay. He was just someone out of my past, with no relevance in my life today.

But then why did my wayward pulse acknowledge his presence with staccato salutes? Dr Menon would of course say that a fluttery pulse was just one more sign of a vata imbalance and perhaps it was an imbalance, just not an Ayurvedic one.

The mind knows it deserves better; it is the heart that forgets.

5

Srinivasan was our instructor for the day, a wiry man who had been at Shanthamaaya for the past four years and could probably get a job as a circus contortionist. He and Kesava took the morning class on alternate days.

Srinivasan said, 'Hari Om and good morning! All newcomers pay attention to the instructions. We are doing first series of shakti bandha asanas today. If you do advance practice at home then stop for now. Many people have problems during ghee time, if anyone has a migraine then tell me and during class they can also do the hare pose and it will help. Okay, let us start.'

The class began with Shalini stumbling through her postures and Srinivasan going over to help her. The yoga teacher had always been particular about paying attention to his female students.

Once I had happened to look around during pranayama, chest violently lifting and falling while practising bhastrika, and I spotted him sitting transfixed at the sight of all our heaving bosoms.

Halfway through the last droning renditions of bhramari, I opened my eyes and discovered that while Srinivasan seemed intrigued by Jenna's unfettered breasts, my ex-husband, sitting cross-legged, seemed to be looking at me in amusement.

He had a smile on his face, not more than a twitch, as I continued making loud buzzing sounds like the mating call of some large, sex-starved bee.

The class began winding down and we finally lay in the corpse pose, focusing on relaxing each part of our body, bit by bit, feet, legs, stomach, fingers, hands, shoulders. Somewhere between concentrating on my upper back and neck, my chronic sleeplessness collapsed on the floor along with the rest of me.

The sun was streaming in through the open windows of the yoga pavilion when I opened my bleary eyes. Jenna, leaning over me, touched my arm and said, 'I thought we should let you sleep for a bit, Anshu. Come, it's breakfast time now.'

I sat up slowly, still groggy. I must have looked decidedly idiotic, I thought, passed out, probably with my mouth open, in the middle of the pavilion. Why on the rare occasion that sleep decided to pay an overdue visit did it have to be in front of my ex-husband and his perfect little wife?

'I wasn't snoring at the end of the class, was I?' I asked Jenna as we walked towards the dining hall.

She tilted her head, the sun turning her hair into a blazing gold, and looked puzzled. 'No, not at all, Anshu. I thought you were just practising corpse pose. It was only when everyone left and you still didn't move that I discovered you were fast asleep.'

Counting my meagre blessings, I entered the dining hall to have our even more meagre breakfast.

~

Enough of apples, I would tell Dr Menon, the least he could do was give me a pear, a guava, anything but another stewed apple, I decided, as I walked towards the clinic for the daily interrogation of 'Are you sweating more or less? Have you passed motions? How many times?' I had to report everything – consistency, colour, texture, everything but taste.

Jay and Shalini were sitting outside the consulting rooms, waiting for their turn. Shalini's self-absorption was evident in the careful manner in which she was applying lip balm on to her thin lips, a mean mouth if you looked at it carefully.

She gave me a swift glance and looked away. I sat on the rattan bench at the other end and picked up the newspaper from the side table, using it more as a shield than as a source of information.

She began talking to her husband, loud enough so that I could just about hear her.

'Is she your age?'

His voice was softer. 'No, much younger.'

'Oh really, in her forties? Surprising really! If this is the result you get by coming here then please it's a nonsense place,' she said with a nasal laugh.

I brought the newspaper down slowly and, ignoring her, looked straight at my ex-husband. He glanced at me apologetically, his cheeks more flushed than usual.

'Raising a young child is very difficult, one must inculcate manners and toilet train them before letting them loose in public spaces,' I said.

'What?' she asked, her face scrunched into a frown.

I folded the paper. 'Oh nothing, just an interesting article about parenting in today's paper. Would you like to read it?' I said, leaning forward with the paper in my hand.

Looking amused, Jay took the paper from me.

'Which page, Anshu?' he asked with twinkling eyes.

'Somewhere in the middle,' I said, smiling back at him.

~

Dr Menon seemed quite pleased with my progress. 'Almost saturated,' he said. A cryptic remark to most, but as a Shanthamaaya veteran, I knew it meant my days of ghee were coming to an end. He sent me to the massage centre. Deepti was on leave and I was handed over to a large woman with a burgeoning moustache and just a smattering of English.

'Namaskaram! Myself Lakshmi, come,' she said, leading me to my regular massage chamber.

She handed me the small, rectangular piece of fabric, little bigger than a sanitary napkin, that I was meant to fasten into a wholly inadequate loincloth before lying down on the wooden pallet.

Lakshmi left the room, drawing a circle around my face with her hands and with a quick 'I come, two minute only' that I deduced meant she was going to fetch the brass plate with incense. This was used as part of the ritual where the masseuse said a small prayer and anointed the forehead with a dot of sandalwood paste before starting the massage.

I undressed and was placing my clothes neatly on the wooden chair when I noticed that across the narrow pond that separated the men's section from ours I could clearly see the corridor that led to the doctors' offices.

My attention was drawn to the massage room opposite, where the larger Russian, Vyacheslav, was having a head massage. One of his family jewels, his tiny Fabergé egg, was peeking out from the left side of his scanty loincloth.

Almost immediately came the startling realization that if they looked across they could see me as well. The window facing the pond did not have the floral blind that normally granted it a modicum of modesty.

Panic-stricken, I looked around the room for something to cover the window. I spotted the blind that for some mysterious reason had been unhooked, rolled over and placed by the sink. The door flew open and Lakshmi walked in with her brass plate.

I desperately tried to make her understand my predicament. Gesturing with my hands as if I was hanging a piece of clothing on a washing line, I said, 'Put blind! Put blind quickly!'

Lakshmi peered at me, a frown on her face, and then calmly placed her palms over her eyes and said, 'Okay madam, I put blind, you no feel shy.' By which time of course Vyacheslav and his moustached attendant were both looking over in delighted glee.

And because trouble usually comes in threes, Jay came sauntering down the corridor and stopped midway, startled, as he too spotted me in my bare-chested, curly bushed glory.

~

Jenna and I were whiling away time, lying under the shade of the kanjiram tree. 'Come, Jenna, it's lunchtime,' I said, shutting my book reluctantly. We walked together under the darkening sky.

'It may rain tonight and it's already pretty windy. Don't forget to keep a sweater handy, we have to keep our bodies warm till purgation tomorrow.'

Purgation was a polite term for violent evacuations of the bowels – the following morning we would both be given the most powerful laxative known to mankind, and spend most of our day rushing to the bathroom.

Shanthamaaya was not for the faint-hearted. If other spas were gentle weekend jogs, this was nothing less than the Ironman Triathlon. We had already been vomiting; otherwise we would have to undergo vamana or induced vomiting. But having dodged that bilious bullet didn't mean we were home free.

After purgation we still had enemas and the esoteric-sounding raktamokshana, where leeches, yes, those slimy, segmented worms with three jaws and hundreds of teeth within their suction cups, attached themselves to us, and blissfully – if only for them – drank our blood.

We sat on a wooden bench, facing the lush gardens while a teal blue kingfisher flitted from one tree to another. Jenna, who usually ate in a distracted manner as if chewing and swallowing were both tedious chores, was wolfing down her khichdi.

She seemed better than she had a few days ago. Dr Menon had been hesitant about interfering in Jenna's treatment, but he had clearly spoken to his colleague, hence the modified diet.

Jenna delicately dabbed away a smear of food from the corner of her mouth and said, 'I was about to come to your room to call you down last night.'

'What happened, Jenna? Were you feeling sick again?'

'No,' she said, 'Lalit – am I saying his name right? He is in the same cottage block as me and was sitting on the patio and watching a movie after dinner last night. He has loads downloaded on his laptop. I thought I would ask you to join us but he said you don't like watching movies. You have met him here before?'

'No, this is his first time at Shanthamaaya, but I know him. He is my ex-husband's cousin. And just a heads-up, if you think Srinivasan is a lech, then let me tell you Lalit would win that competition hands down.'

Jenna shrugged. 'Really? They both seem so harmless.' She seemed to have a lack of awareness about her body and of others around her, which I found both endearing and worrying. I was not sure if Jenna had noticed the male staff at Shanthamaaya, or even the other patients, staring at her unencumbered breasts.

'I want Srinivasan to teach me how to perform a few asanas. I want to incorporate them into a piece I am planning.' Jenna pulled out a notebook from her jhola. 'This, how do you say this?'

'Pungu Mayurasana,' I read in her meticulously neat handwriting. 'The Wounded Peacock.'

'Yes, I would like to attempt a recreation of a famous piece from the sixties by Yoko Ono. She sat fully clothed and the audience was invited to come forward and cut pieces of her clothes. They started hesitantly, first just a piece from the sleeve, from the collar, but eventually they pulled at her till her clothes were reduced to rags. I want to do a variant while holding this pose. A contemplation on how when we wound people we are truly wounding ourselves.'

'And you are all right with people cutting your clothes off?'

It was the first time I had seen the diffident, unsure young woman completely animated. 'Anshu, when I am performing, my body is just an instrument, a way to convey and evoke emotions. There is a certain dissociation between my physical self and the person within.'

By the time she finished explaining all the aspects of the piece it was too late to backtrack and tell her that the ex-husband I had referred to was Jay, which, if I were honest, was a bit of a relief. The thought of people knowing, staring, comparing me to Shalini, sending sympathetic glances my way, was abhorrent to me.

~

There was a musical programme that night. On a raised platform under a painted dome with depictions of peacocks and marigolds sat three mundu-clad men with instruments.

I had settled on a seat next to Jenna when Shalini strode towards the row ahead of us, Jay, Lalit and Vivaan in tow, and took her seat.

The programme began with a plump flautist in a tight black shirt that he had incongruously paired with a saffron mundu. He was accompanied by the tabla player and another young boy, whose only musical abilities seemed to lie in the esoteric field of clapping his hands to the beat.

I felt as if a tapeworm were crawling into my ear and eating its way into my brain. Forty-five painful minutes later, the programme came to an end to enthusiastic applauding, primarily by the boy who had been clapping rhythmically. Next up, after a ten-minute break, there was a lecture by Dr Pillai on 'dosha management'.

Jay, in a bid to entertain himself – or perhaps having decided that rather than ignoring each other's presence for the next few weeks, it was more convenient for him to pretend that we were long-lost buddies – brought up the humiliating morning escapade in the sly manner so typical of him.

'Anshu,' he called out, 'you used to be such a meticulous gardener, but I believe now you have given it all up. The patch is all straggly weeds and curly creepers waving hello in the breeze!'

I knew exactly what patch he was referring to and my cheeks began burning. I was embarrassed not as much by him seeing me naked as by him seeing me in my hairy, Neanderthal form.

But a part of me also felt like laughing at the subversive pleasure he seemed to find in bringing this up in front of Shalini, especially after she had been so obnoxious that morning. He was like a schoolboy throwing paper airplanes under the teacher's nose.

Shalini did not react. This seemingly innocuous conversation about horticulture was of no interest to her.

Her head, with its expertly streaked gold highlights which unfortunately in Kerala's humidity and Shanthamaaya's hairdryer-free policy had turned into a blonde frizz, remained bent over the magazine in her lap.

The kind of woman who spent most of her life between grooming and preening, she had probably lasered everything off till I am sure hers, unlike mine, resembled an eight-year-old's crotch.

In the good old days, I had made a little more effort, with just a landing strip to give directions, but lately it had seemed like too much work.

'Once I go back, I will restore my garden to its regular neatness as I entertain many visitors there now. Thank you for your concern,' I said airily.

Which of course brought a broad grin on to his face and sounded utterly ridiculous, unlike in my head where it had seemed dismissively witty.

Only then did I notice that Vivaan was peering at me like he had caught on that this was more than a banal garden-variety exchange.

6

The next afternoon, while I was feeling like I had excreted all the solids from my body including my organs, Dr Menon came to visit me in my room.

'How many times have you been to the bathroom?' he asked, with a pleased smile on his face as if I was a toddler he was potty training.

'I stopped counting after the first fourteen times, doctor, but it seems to have stopped now.'

He checked my pulse carefully and declared that I was all purged out and free to leave the confines of my room.

After a hot shower and half a bowl of rice kanji in my stomach, I pulled out a sling bag and stuffed two back-dated issues of the *New Yorker* that some long-departed patient had left behind. A stroll, I thought, past the vegetable gardens and into the woods, would make for a refreshing change after being chained to the bathroom for most of the day.

An old cashmere shawl, fuzzy and pilling with age, which could double up as a pillow if I found the perfect tree to lie beneath, went into my jhola along with a bottle of water. If I had the strength, I decided, I would even walk as far as the stream that I had stumbled upon on another idle afternoon, years ago.

It was drizzling, more a warm, damp mist than rain. In the centre of the ornate porch stood Jay, struggling to open an umbrella.

He looked up at my approach, giving me a self-deprecating shrug as I walked towards him. He had always been hopeless with mechanical things. Contrary to his swaggering demeanour, he could barely change the batteries in a remote control.

'Let me see,' I said, taking the umbrella from him.

'I didn't know it rained in Kerala at this time, Anshu.'

'April showers, Jay. The forecast says moderate to heavy rainfall for the next few weeks, which is good actually after two successive monsoon failures.'

One of the prongs was bent. I straightened it out and the umbrella popped open.

'Shit! How did you do that!' he asked as I handed him the umbrella.

'I think the umbrella just likes me more than you. You have a treatment at the clinic, Jay?'

'No,' he said, 'I am going to Lalit's room.'

We didn't notice Vivaan walking towards us till he called out. He asked, 'Anshu, where have you been? I haven't seen you all day.' Before I could answer, Jay said, 'It was her purgation day. Right?'

I nodded and Vivaan, taking in my bag and Jay's open umbrella, asked, 'Where are you all off to, the Prince?'

'Jay is going to meet Lalit,' I said, adding that I was going for a leisurely stroll behind the yoga pavilion. 'There is a beautiful walking path there flanked by fruit trees, almost a forest of sapodilla and jackfruit. It's a far more scenic view than seeing the trucks and cows on the main road.'

Vivaan leaned back against the railing. 'If you are fine with some dull company, Anshu, then I don't mind tagging along. I haven't been to that side of the property.'

Jay butted in, 'It's raining, Vivaan. You are aware that you shouldn't get wet and cold before purgation, no?'

'Oh right, yes. I attended that lecture by Dr Pillai, "Otherwise the ghee will congeal inside". A vivid mental picture indeed.' Vivaan laughed as he located another umbrella in the far corner, and said, 'There! Problem solved!'

There was a queer imbalance that had come sweeping into the porch along with a gust of wind. I pushed my hair away from my face and spoke a little too quickly, bending my head slightly to get under Vivaan's umbrella.

'Come, Vivaan, I will show you the organic garden along the way. But you know, Jay is right, you must tell me if you feel chilly, I have something that will keep you warm.'

A whip cloaked within his mocking tone, Jay asked, 'And what are you planning on keeping him warm with, Anshu, your arms?'

With a laugh that sounded distinctly false even to my ears, I said, 'I don't think I will have to resort to such drastic measures, Jay. Luckily I have a shawl in my bag.'

I did not know whether Lalit had told Vivaan about our history together, but rather than turning this into a sideshow, with us, the star performers, knocking each other on the head with our juggling balls, I turned and walked down the steps.

Vivaan, who looked confused at this unexpected turn to our exchange, followed me, till he was close enough to cover both our heads under the striped umbrella.

By evening, the misty drizzle changed to a grey sheet of rain. There was a celebratory dinner that night, a reward for stoically bearing the rigours of purgation. After days of rice kanji, bland vegetables and boiled dal, I was going to be served what seemed to be the equivalent of a Kathakali performance on my tongue, piping hot onion uttappams.

Vivaan and I had reached the dining room late. My clothes were still damp from our walk, though I had made sure that Vivaan stayed warm with my shawl wrapped around his shoulders despite his many protests.

I was looking around for a table when Jenna, who was sitting at the far end with Jay, Shalini and Lalit, called out to us. Vivaan strode towards their table. I reluctantly followed him and took a seat.

Dipping a piece of my uttappam in green chutney, I noticed that Lalit was staring at my chest, as if there was a slogan emblazoned across my kurta.

I looked down. The rain had turned my kurta transparent in parts and, to make matters worse, I had been casually leaning against the table unaware that my breasts were resting on it like musk melons on display. I hastily took the napkin from my lap and tucked it into my collar, like I was a three-year-old who had forgotten her bib.

My ex-husband, who had first looked at us with distaste as we approached their table, now seemed to be enjoying himself, watching my discomfort, a sardonic twist to his lips.

'How is the uttappam, good?' he asked.

'Yes, delicious, thank you.'

Shalini, her eyebrows raised, laughed mockingly. 'So nice, so civilized, Biwi No. 1 and Biwi No. 2 both together in one place, at one table.'

Lalit, who perhaps, like her, believed that making people deeply uncomfortable was a bloody good joke, began guffawing. She was encouraged by his reaction and gleefully raised a hand for a high-five. 'But Lalit, come on, be honest, No. 2 is better than No. 1, right?'

Jay and I both spoke at once. His 'Stop it, Shalini!' and my 'Actually it depends on how full of shit one is!' overlapped each other. She looked at me, confusion written all over her face, the jibe once again incomprehensible to her.

Jay and I instinctively exchanged glances. I rolled my eyes for a second and he, pulling his lips together, holding back a smile, nodded almost imperceptibly. These were swift, tiny movements, unnoticeable unless someone was paying minute attention.

There had been countless crowded parties and innumerable work dinners where we had made similar exchanges. A raised eyebrow, a look in the eye that meant 'save me from this bore'. A shake of the head that said 'it's time to leave'. All couples develop such wordless codes. I sat back disconcerted. How had we slipped back into this routine so dexterously, so comfortably?

Jenna, who had barely been able to follow the

conversation, asked what Biwi No. 1 meant. Keeping my head down, pretending to be engrossed in my food, I said, 'Me. Shalini is talking about me. Biwi No. 1 means first wife. Jay is my ex-husband. Fine, Shalini, happy?'

I ordered one more uttappam. I was not going to leave the first decent meal I had been served, the one I had looked forward to all these days, because of her. My gaze fixed to the plate, I continued eating in silence.

But the evening didn't end there. Shanthamaaya, in trying to keep its occupants occupied so they forgot at least in part about their growling stomachs, had a series of programmes after dinner. The dismal musical show had only been the beginning. A trataka class had also been organized for us.

There were only five of us waiting in the pavilion for the class to begin. The Russians, primarily interested in losing weight, were missing and so was Javed, though Anil had already taken a seat on the floor.

Pam and Glenda with a 'You must come along, Lalit!' had stewarded him to the library, ostensibly to play backgammon. But I was convinced they were more interested in sharing the contents of his steel thermos. In a distinctly un-Christlike manner, he had boasted that he had converted his dosha-calming water to Sula's Sauvignon Blanc.

Sreenivasan had us kneeling on cushions around a low table. A single candle in the middle.

'Resting the gaze on a single point, the restless mind also finds a place to rest. I will switch the lights off and then you begin. No blinking, if you feel like blinking, close the eyes and focus on the afterimage of the flame,' he said in the resigned manner of a man who had said the same words repeatedly for years.

The room was filled with darkness, the steady flame the only illumination. We had just begun when Shalini said, 'Oof, this is too boring, Jay, let's go!' Sreenivasan, standing at the far left, switched the lights back on.

'Madam, please don't disrupt the class!' Anil, annoyed at the interruption, also gave off a big sigh.

A frown marred Shalini's immaculately tweezed eyebrows. 'What's your problem, dude?' she asked Anil and not wanting to get into a confrontation he simply shook his head. 'Come, Jay, let's go to our room.'

My ex-husband, his spine erect, remained still, in perfect vajrasana, though his face reflected the irritation evident in his low voice as he said in a harsh whisper, 'Shalini, stop it, you are disturbing everyone. Either you do the class quietly or go to the room.'

I was watching Shalini, her recoil at the rebuke, her eyes quickly meeting mine, perhaps to see if I had witnessed what she felt was her abasement. She stood up and in a swift movement left the pavilion. The meshed door slammed behind her, and the sudden blast of air that came in snuffed the flame.

There was an embarrassed silence in the room till Sreenivasan said, 'Sorry for the disturbance, let us begin now.' After relighting the candle, he plunged the room into partial darkness once again.

'If thoughts appear, let them come, let them go, but keep your eyes on the candle flame,' Sreenivasan intoned in his singsong manner.

The need to blink made my eyes water, till finally I closed them. And when I opened my eyes again for the next round, I saw Jay was watching me, his gaze fixed, unwavering.

The diffused light stripped the years away from him. I could see the man from my youth sitting across another candlelit table, across time itself, the man who made me laugh as he inadvertently mispronounced bidet, which became my pet name for him for a few years.

Bibet, I used to call him, and he in turn called me Juju, an abbreviation for jujube, a small fruit that tasted like a mix of apples and dates.

I glanced back at the candle but couldn't stop my gaze from repeatedly sliding back to him.

When Sreenivasan finally switched the lights on and declared that the trataka class had come to an end, Jay ambled over to the window to get a glass of water from the earthen pot.

He turned towards me and said, 'Anshu, wait, I want to talk to you for a second.' Vivaan and Jenna were waiting for me near the door, but I waved them onward and walked towards my ex-husband.

'I just want to say I am sorry, she had no business making all those statements, even at the clinic, I really don't know what to say.'

'It's all right, Jay, everyone would have got to know sooner or later, I guess. I just wish I'd had the opportunity of choosing when to tell them myself.'

'I can only apologize on her behalf, Anshu. She's not easy to handle but I am going to talk to her.'

'It's all right,' I repeated, bending down to fill a glass from the dispenser.

The water was warm, my hand unsteady as I gulped it down, and a trickle splattered on to my kurta. I was raising my arm to wipe my mouth, when he caught my hand. 'You still have this?'

A tiny circle of gold, a wreath wrapped around my finger. It was not my wedding band – that I had discarded a long time ago. This was my first present from Jay. I looked up at him, the memory intertwined in my mind with the lunch we had consumed that day. Chinese, at a hole in the wall called 'Stomach'.

Jay had dropped toothpicks into the chicken Schezwan and then summoned the manager to get us lunch on the house. We left the restaurant giggling, thrilled with our prank, promising to carry dead cockroaches and flies wrapped in tissue paper and stuffed into our pockets on our next date.

We crossed the road and I looked into the store window behind me, Motiwala or Minawala, the name of the store was the one thing I could not recall clearly, and I saw the gold ring. He bought it for me.

'Do you remember,' he said, his voice echoing in the empty yoga pavilion, 'once in the middle of a fight, you threw it over the wall of your house? And after we made up, we jumped into your neighbour's garden, scrambling on our hands and knees, looking for it in the grass?'

He smiled, not letting go of my hand. 'We found it in some plant, right?'

'Yes, it had fallen into a marigold pot.'

Almost two decades had passed but I recalled that evening distinctly.

'You took me for a long drive then and when we returned Mummy was waiting for us at the door in her favourite striped nightgown, the one that said "I love Mickey Mouse", you remember that? She screamed, "You are a thief!" and when I asked her, "But what have I stolen, Mummy?" she yelled back, "You have stolen time! You had to come back at eleven. Now it's twelve-thirty. This is robbery only of full one and a half hours!'"

He laughed. He had an odd laugh, four precise beats and then it was over, rehearsed, almost theatrical. He once told me that he used to stammer when he was very young and he would constantly practise his speech, stretching out the vowels when he was in the bathroom.

I could picture him, a young boy standing in front of the mirror, rehearsing various words and probably this very laugh after brushing his teeth every night. My heart swelled for the little lost boy that I knew was still lurking there inside. I looked down at the ring, my hand still clasped within his, and I said, 'I am used to it on my hand, some things become a habit.'

We walked back together to the main building, ghosts in rustling white, walking in the darkness, unhurried, both making a tally of the things we had lost, things that would never be found at the bottom of flower pots.

7

Another morning, another predawn class. Shanthamaaya did not seem to believe that variety was the spice of life. Instead, it both figuratively and literally served the blandest, most monotonous food on the planet.

Kesava's reedy voice echoed in the wooden pavilion: 'Now we will perform Natarajasan. Bend right leg backward and hold your right ankle with right hand. Extend left arm straight, your palm faces the ground.'

'I think you should just do a facepalm instead,' I said to a frustrated Vivaan, who had been struggling with various asanas from the beginning of the class. He shook his head and, with a determined look on his face, balanced his weight on his left leg and lifted his right leg in the air.

A few seconds later he lost balance and his flailing arm banged into mine. Still groggy from yet another night of constant awakenings, I tumbled and clattered into Jenna on my right. The three of us went spiralling on to the floor in a burst of decidedly un-yogic groans and giggles.

Lalit ignored Vivaan, though he was the one who had been standing closest to him, and went scrambling to lift Jenna up, treating her as if she was a helpless old woman instead of a twenty-seven-year-old gymnast.

I punched Vivaan on the arm and whispered, 'Couldn't you have fallen to your left and crushed Lalit instead?'

He stood up, chivalrously giving me his hand for support, and smiled. 'It's a problem I have, Anshu, I like doing things only the right way.'

Kesava's stern 'No chit-chatting here!' rang through the pavilion. Feeling guilty about disrupting the class, I quickly got on to my stomach for the next pose. It was shalabhasana, the locust pose. I had to raise my head and look straight ahead, which meant this time Jay and I were facing each other, holding the pose, holding each other's gaze.

My eyes traced the planes of his face, the precisely angled bones. Time had softened some of the decisive lines, a blurring akin to rubbing a thumb over a charcoal drawing. But unlike most long-term smokers, he had been spared a certain grim decline. His skin was still ruddy, if slightly creased, largely devoid of bags and pouches, of the weathered luggage we tend to accumulate with age. 'Now, change to matsya kridasana, flapping fish pose,' said Kesava, and we turned away from each other.

~

After two failed attempts at trying to call my sister as I walked towards the Prince, I sent her a message.

Pick up!

And almost immediately came the reply.

Can't. Running late- Ok am lesbian.

My head bent over the phone, I smiled and typed back quickly.

What! And you just found out? Omg! have you told mummy?

A minute later she wrote back.

No! am lesbian not lesbian

A lungi-clad man passed me in the opposite direction, looking at me curiously as I laughed out aloud while deciding to pull my sister's leg just a bit longer.

Is this an existential question like 'to be or not to be'? ok get it, you are bisexual –cool!

Mandira's reply made me laugh even louder, her fury evident in the capital letters.

Hate my phone! bloody autocorrect – AM LEAVING – not AM LESBIAN, you idiot!

I was still smiling to myself when I saw Jay standing at the small shop by the Prince, buying some gum.

'Chewing gum is against Shanthamaaya's principles,' I said as I passed him.

He reached out for me with one hand, holding my arm. 'Hang on, you have some change? This fellow doesn't have enough,' he said, holding a five-hundred-rupee note in his hand. I rummaged in my jhola and took out a few tens.

'One bottle of water, right?' he asked me. 'And one coffee, milk and sugar on the side,' Jay said to the server at the Prince as we took our seats.

He adjusted his chair, bringing it closer to the table.

'So tell me, how have things been with you, Anshu?' he asked. 'Are you still teaching at Harmony?'

'Not for the last four years. I have my own playschool now, Toddler's Academy. It's in Andheri and I have a second branch opening in Santacruz this August,' I said and then began worrying that I may have sounded like I was bragging, though my intention had been to merely show him that I had done well enough without him.

'Really? I didn't know that, Anshu.' His eyes steady, he conducted an appraisal of some sort and perhaps satisfied with the conclusion he nodded. 'I have to say that I am impressed. You seem to have really flourished.'

'And you? Have you left the private banking world for what everyone seems to be into these days – a start-up?'

'No, still a humble wealth-manager-cum-slave at IIFL but I think this year I will finally branch out on my own.'

He took out a packet of Marlboros from his kurta pocket, and leisurely lit one.

'If Dr Menon could see you now, he would collapse,' I said. 'Chewing gum, coffee, smoking, all three are not allowed, you know.'

'Yes, I remember the rules from the last time I came here with you.'

'And now you are here with Biwi No. 2.'

'Yes,' he said with a snort. He shook his head. 'And what a big mistake it has turned out to be, bringing her here, she hates everything about it.'

'It's not everyone's cup of ghee,' I said, laughing at my own pun.

His head tilted to the left, the sunlight making him squint, narrowing his eyes. 'It's nice to see you happy, Anshu.'

'It's nice to see you happy too, Jay,' I said, feeling like we were both playing a part.

He smiled, a cynical, weary smile. 'You really think I look happy?' And at that moment, Jay looked his age, all his fifty-two years visible in those drained, grey eyes.

'Aren't you?' I asked.

There was no answer. He moved his hand forward and placed it over my right hand, gently, his fingers moving up and down. He was quiet, looking down, and after a few moments he said, 'Your skin is so smooth, Anshu, has always been.'

His hands had a multitude of freckles, like a page out of the joining the dots worksheets we gave out at Toddler's.

'Brown skin ages better than your wannabe Caucasian kind,' I said.

'Still the same Juju. Always ready with a quick answer.'

Juju. Like a tuning fork when struck. An unfaltering tone from the distant past, louder between us than the sounds of a passing truck, the fan overhead, my phone ringing in my jhola as we sat at the table, my hand enclosed within his.

His coffee arrived and with a shrug, almost absent-mindedly, like he had not quite realized his hand was still over mine, he moved it away.

~

The plastic dispenser in the corner was leaking, one drop at a time splattering on to the cream and green tiled floor, a puddle forming next to my left foot. Leaning against a wooden pillar that faced the narrow pond, I was waiting for Dr Menon once again.

In the twenty-first century there are as many doctors as there are ailments. Tone-deaf cardiologists who listen to irregular heartbeats but can't hear a heartbreak. Oncologists who don't know that cancer erupted in the breast because a strong emotion was smothered within, jaded gynaecologists peering at a conveyor belt of arid vaginas, prescriptions of K-Y Jelly in their hands, not realizing that the problem lies in the lack of love and not the lack of lubrication.

Doctors treating symptoms and not the organism, looking at us like we are part of a factory assembly line, each component constructed with the same exacting specifications. But aren't we more like matryoshka dolls? One layer nesting within another. Even when you think you have come to the final doll, strip us down to our skeleton and you will find yet another nesting inside, invisible, unseen.

Inside Dr Menon's clinic, all the dolls were extracted, stacked up in a line and examined for dents and scratches.

I entered the consulting room for our daily briefing and sat on the high-backed chair, facing the window, across the desk from where he presided in his dignified cream silk.

I was not looking at him. I didn't have the strength to squint into the sunlight, and preferred looking down at the floor, tracing the hexagonal pattern repeatedly with my toe.

It is difficult to befriend the present when you are

still quarrelling with the past. And I had spent the night getting sucker-punched. My body jerking repeatedly as I would fall asleep, startling me awake instantly.

'Anshu,' Dr Menon said, his voice a low timbre, soothing, like balm on an aching forehead, 'what is bothering you?'

I had recently been to a counsellor, a curly-haired Parsi woman with gold spectacles perched over her aquiline nose. She thought an exercise, something she did with children, would be helpful. A safe place was what she called it.

Each time I woke up at night, my heart pounding after a twitch or a jerk, I had to close my eyes and imagine my safe place. Somewhere that I felt calm, that didn't hold unpalatable emotions.

This room with its clean, cream walls, wooden ceiling and this learned man with laughing eyes, sitting across me, constituted my safe place. The one I had begun disappearing to from my four-poster bed at home time and again.

So I told him. 'I have spent the night trying not to think about the things that I don't want to think about!'

'Anshu, but if we bury things without truly addressing them, they will keep calling us again and again, isn't it?'

'I have buried them, doctor, that should be enough. They are memories, not vampires that I need to say, "Take this, sire!" before running a stake through their hearts.'

An exhalation and I continued, 'I think it's Jay being here that is making my symptoms worse, that's all. I was fine till he arrived.'

'I know you are upset that he is here, Anshu, but look at it as an opportunity to finally resolve things within you. Your burying hasn't worked, has it? Otherwise why would his presence here disturb you? Loss doesn't just disappear. We have to work to replace it with hard-won emotional accomplishments or it turns into our greatest adversaries, despair and fear.'

'And those ashwagandha pills you have given me? Do they help despair flee in fright?'

He chuckled at my poor attempt at making a joke before nodding. 'Yes.'

'And love?' I asked with a wry smile.

Dr Menon looked confused.

'A pill to drive away love, doctor?'

'Anshu, that is a job for witch doctors, it is out of the hands of us poor Ayurveda ones. But what I think may just help you is shirodhara. I will put you down at 11 a.m. for a session.'

Dr Menon made some notations in my file.

'One day I will steal this file and see what all you have written down about me over the years. But knowing my luck, it will end up being in that squiggly, barely legible handwriting that all you doctors so proudly adopt.'

He shook his head with a smile that lit up his entire face. 'No, worse, it's in Malayalam.'

~

There were bugs all over the dining hall because of the drizzle. One had just drowned in my leftover sambar. I had polished off two dosas and was leaning back in my chair satiated. Madhu, her lipstick smeared around her mouth as she absent-mindedly patted her lips with a napkin, was telling us about her Babaji's many accurate predictions.

'I am telling you, he is too good. Come, Vivaan. You show Babaji your palm and he will tell you so many things about yourself that you will be amazed!'

Babaji put his roti down and moved his arm towards Vivaan's fork-wielding hand. Vivaan at first pulled his hand back but then seemed to change his mind. 'Babaji, I have also studied palmistry. Will you please allow me to read your palm first?'

Vivaan grasped the pandit's outstretched arm and turned his palm towards him. Babaji was taken aback but couldn't find a way out.

Vivaan peered intently at Babaji's fingers, at the lines that cut across the palm. He turned his hand at different angles trying to catch the light from the overhead brass lamp.

'Babaji, do you have a strong connection with the moon?'

Babaji looked hesitant and then he merely nodded. Vivaan, his eyes squinting in concentration, scrutinized the palm again. 'Does your name start with the letter A?'

Madhu gave a squeal of excitement. 'Yes it does!'

By this time the other residents, having finished their dinner, had started gathering around our table. Vivaan flipped Babaji's palm back and forth a few more times. 'I can see some connection with mountains in your hand – do you live close to one?'

Before Babaji could reply, Vivaan said, 'And this I don't have to ask you but your hand clearly tells me, Babaji, you are from Indore! Am I right?'

Babaji's astonishment could not be concealed any more and out came a squeaky 'Yes, it is right.' Disentangling his hand from Vivaan's and cradling it as if it was injured, Babaji burst out, 'Jai Sri Krishna, you are a very talented person. How many years have you studied palmistry?'

'Too many to count, Babaji!'

With a muttered 'Ram Ram!' Babaji hurriedly left the table and Madhu, who seemed to want to stay back, had no recourse but to excuse herself as well.

Lalit, who had been leaning over Jenna's chair, sat down on the empty one beside her. He had been watching the proceedings with great interest. He extended his palm now. 'Vivaan yaar, read my palm also, but tell me just the good things, like "You will live till you are ninety, surrounded by Playboy bunnies à la Hugh Hefner." I don't want to know any of that "From the months of January to October you will be in poor health." Some fortune teller said this to my first wife once! From the time she stubbed her toe the following day she would keep muttering about how she had to get through this bad period for the next six months.'

Vivaan looked at his hand and was about to say something, but then he burst out laughing. 'Lalit, I don't know any palmistry!'

I looked at him confused, and he said, 'Arrey, when I went to fill in my details in the guest register, right above my name I saw Babaji's details in bold letters. It said, Pandit Amit Chand Joshi, Mountain View Apartments, Indore. If you have a habit of reading everything you get your hands on, then reading hands also becomes easy!'

Recalling Babaji's shocked face, his eyes widening with each of Vivaan's proclamations, I was seized with uncontrollable laughter.

I don't know if it was because my stomach was full of delicious dosas, or because I could not remember the last time I had laughed till my chest ached. Perhaps it was the intimacy that quickly creeps up between people when they are locked away together for a period of time, like on those reality shows like *Bigg Boss* or *Survivor*. But impulsively I leaned across the table and gave Vivaan a kiss on the cheek.

Wiping away my tears of mirth, I told him what I had been meaning to say to him all this time: 'You really are a remarkable man, Vivaan!'

~

My relic-filled mind was a godown and these tired eyelids the rolling shutters that had rusted halfway down. They did not open easily nor did they roll down and shut.

Instead of further futile attempts to sleep, I made a few more to-do lists in my yellow diary, the one that proclaimed 'Eat, Drink, Live' and right below, a scalding 'Oh Shut Up Fatty!'

I then leaned back, looking down at my hands, the clipped nails with white spots, a new one on the thumbnail. Lack of calcium, my grandmother used to say. She was wrong. Milk spots are a collection of injuries, some seemingly so insignificant that we don't register them happening; but bludgeons we have forgotten also leave a mark.

That afternoon when I returned from the spa building after yet another distressing treatment, I had a visitor.

'Can I come in?' Jay asked.

Perhaps it was the talk I had had with Dr Menon the other day about stakes and hearts, but his waiting to be invited in reminded me of vampire stories. The ghoul can't cross the threshold till he is asked inside and when the gullible soul nods, the way I instinctively did, the vampire is free to enter, sink his fangs in and suck his victim dry.

We remained standing. The room smaller than it had been a moment ago, as if we were inside a deflating balloon, the air slowly leaking out. I opened the wooden window shutters, the left one grazing my fingers as I pulled it towards me. I turned and stood with my back against the meshed opening.

'That Vivaan,' he began without preamble, 'how old is he – twenty-nine, thirty?'

'We have not discussed his age,' I said as I pushed my hair away from my face, twisting it into a loose knot. 'We have other things to talk about, Jay.'

'Oh yes? So what do you talk to him about constantly? Do you know how silly you look, giggling at everything he says, giving him kisses! Or is all this to get a reaction out of me, Anshu – is that what your game is all about?'

A game. If anything, I had been playing hide-and-seek with myself. I had looked for people, not just Vivaan but Jenna as well, people to hide inside, throw myself into, bury my head within them like a pair of headphones.

Their words a buffer against the white noise of loneliness that seemed to have got louder since Jay came here.

When I didn't reply he took a step closer.

'Do you remember,' he asked, 'when we went to Prague? We stayed at that hotel, what was it called, some converted monastery?'

'Augustine,' I said.

'And from the main station you said that tram no. 22 would bring us back to the hotel and I said that it was tram no. 18, and I would reach before you? Do you remember that? And when you reached the hotel, I was already standing at the tram station waiting for you?'

'Yes, I remember.'

'I never took the other tram, Anshu. When you climbed into the compartment, I waved at you and then walked all the way back and got into another compartment. You didn't see me but I was in the same tram as you. I could see you, sitting ahead, your head against the window.'

His hand was on my cheek now. 'This,' he said, 'this feels like the same, being on the tram, in a different compartment, still looking at you.'

When I didn't answer, he said, 'You do remember Prague, don't you? It was a great holiday.'

I recalled the trip differently. We would climb aboard the dented red trams each day. He would argue about which one to take. 'Tram no. 7,' he insisted once. Ten minutes later, he made me change to tram no. 11. It took us to the outskirts of the city and at my insistence he agreed to get off so we could head back before we got lost any further.

A tall girl with a blonde ponytail asked us the way to Petrin Gardens and he, the ever-gallant knight, took the map from my hand and began giving elaborate directions.

We climbed aboard another tram, the neighbourhood getting seedier and seedier with every stop. He decided to get off and looked at the signboard at the station, trying to figure out where we were.

'We are at a station called Zákaz Kouření,' he said, 'look for it on the map.' I did not have the heart to tell him 'Zákaz Kouření' was written at every stop and was not the name of any station but just meant 'no smoking'.

I saw people on Segways, whizzing up and down, the new-age way of seeing a city. 'Let's try a guided Segway tour instead, Jay.'

He laughed. 'Let's not forget how clumsy you can be, you'll just end up breaking both your legs.'

Just then I saw a family of South Indians with a sari-clad grandma going by on their Segways, sparse white hair escaping her helmet and flying in the wind.

Another morning. Sitting on the bed wrapped in a fluffy, pristine white towel that only hotels seem to have,

I tried kissing him. He let me, a perfunctory gesture. Our mouths did not seem to fit together, like pieces of mismatched puzzles mixed together, forgotten in a toy box and then pulled out haphazardly. It had been near the end, sizes, edges, patterns, nothing seemed to match.

His hand moved from my cheek towards my coiled bun, unknotting it. A tug, but of what? Pain? Pleasure? All mixed together, like khichdi stirred together into a mush, unable to differentiate the lentils from the rice.

He liked my hair open, always had. Wanting to please him in those days, I gave up countless things – thinking that the more I did things the way he liked, he would have to like me more and more as well. Ponytails and French braids were just minor casualties.

A stream of words ran through my head, an unexpected anger at my own subservience. What was I doing? Was I his pet bitch? Heel, stay, chase the ball, come, lick and then roll over and play dead.

But the words went unheeded. The nebulous line between should and did had caused many wars greater than the one in my mind.

His hand stayed in my hair. I didn't stop him. I had always been fixated on Jay. Because he had been the first. Not a lover – that crown belonged to a lanky boy who in the midst of our clumsy fumbling, along with other things, had managed to get our braces entangled as well.

But the first in every other way. His nose brushed against my ear, that goddamn perfect nose that could be on a Roman coin.

He said fetch.

I said woof.

8

We went on an excursion. A boat ride around the lake had been organized for all the patients. Clear water, fish swimming around weeds, a partially submerged temple in the middle, darkened with time to a patina of lead grey.

Shalini had decided to give the outing a miss. 'How dull!' she declared and tried persuading her husband to go to the Prince, but Lalit had agreed to accompany her instead.

Dr Pillai, sitting at the bow, pointed out a trailing green stem with yellow flowers. 'That's called, pith, *Aeschynomene aspera*, we use it for coughs and the dried shoot is sometimes powdered and administered to improve the consistency of semen.'

Jay was seated next to me, and I was acutely aware of his cotton-clad leg pressed against mine.

'Have you noticed that Dr Pillai is always talking about reproduction in some form or the other?' Jay said softly.

'What do you expect, Bibet? I believe he has five children so he is clearly an expert in that field if not in any other,' I whispered back.

My ex-husband said, 'Bibet! It's been a long time since I have heard that,' and smiled his lopsided grin, the one that reached those equanimous eyes and dawdled there like the last guest to leave a party.

It had all begun again, I suppose, that afternoon when he had come to my room.

We had started finding places to meet, holding hands under the table when we sat in groups for meals, spending all day practising a version of trataka, except we could blink at will.

We would gaze at each other across dining rooms, over doctors' heads, across lotus ponds and behind Shalini's back.

I would be smiling at something Vivaan said as we took our daily strolls around the garden together or making a mess of the paints and canvas with Jenna on the front porch, but each time Jay looked at me, my head would fill with memories.

A river rafting trip, where I fell overboard. A hotel room in Agra where we tied each other up much before

Fifty Shades of Grey. The cake he would bake for me every birthday, sometimes gooey, at other times with the texture of a thermocol sheet.

A trip to Mont Saint Michel, where Jay forgot to shut the window and I woke up covered with black insects. We had to rush to the local hospital where the doctor holding a syringe in his hand said, 'Don't worry, this will just be a small prick.' I remember cracking up, tears in my eyes, laughing uncontrollably, saying, 'Doctor, this is the only time when a woman will tell you a small prick is better than a big one!'

Jay's staccato laugh, as I clutched on to his hand and turned my face away so I would not see the needle going in.

The linearity of time scrambled, looping back upon itself like the chakris we used to burn at Diwali, one spark and it was set ablaze, the universe spinning.

~

A blue bus full of tourists on their way to Vadakkunnathan temple for Thrissur Pooram had stopped at the Prince that afternoon. The place was a kaleidoscope of colourful saris and bawling children clamouring for toffees and lollipops from the adjacent small shop. The air was filled with the smell of pomfret moilee and naadan beef fry.

The sacred cow had no relevance here in Kerala, unlike in the rest of the country where they would have burned the Prince down and slaughtered the grey-haired man who had just finished his lunch, his blue checked shirt stained with beef curry.

When I repeated this to my sister on the phone, she said, 'It would serve them right!' Sometimes I wondered if we had both had the same upbringing; at other times I was certain that this was her stocky husband's influence on her.

I thought she was going to badger me again about Jay. But she had something else on her mind that afternoon. 'Do you think Mummy has the hots for that Khurana Uncle? Have you met him? She seems to talk about him a lot these days,' she said with a snort.

My sister, like most people, believed that a woman of a certain age and especially her mother should be satisfied playing a delineated role, going to kirtans, sending laddoos for her grandchildren. Her shopping trolley should never have push-up bras and lace negligees, but must hold discounted detergent and cough syrup almost past its sell-by date – just like her.

For more than two decades, Mummy's life had followed the same pattern. Card sessions every afternoon at Khar Gymkhana for precisely three hours except

Fridays, when she would go to Lata's parlour to set her hair. This was an architectural monument of curls, frozen in place with litres of Elnett hairspray.

If a bee entered Mummy's beehive, it would be instantly exterminated and its corpse found only a week later, when she returned to the parlour to wash and set her hair again.

But something had changed recently. She stayed back at the club later these days and one afternoon I discovered Luv Khurana sitting quietly next to Mummy in our flat, a glass of cold Rooh Afza in his hand.

'Yes, he came home once.'

'What is he like?'

'He was in the army, has a bald head and calls everyone "dear". "Dear, how are you?" "Dear, get me a glass of water." Like he was about to start dictating a letter but forgot your name!'

With an unsure note in her voice, Mandira asked, 'You think at this age she has found a boyfriend?'

'Maybe they are just fuck-buddies,' I said.

'Eww, Anshu! How can you even say things like that!'

'Dear, why do you ask me such stupid things then!' I laughed.

At which point Mandy said Mummy was on call waiting, and put all three of us on conference call.

'Mummy, Mandy wants to really ask you something urgently,' I said. My sister was silent but quickly recovered with, 'Nothing, Mummy, I sent you those pictures on WhatsApp, the plain brown bag or the one covered with LV logos, which one should I get for my ma-in-law's birthday? She gives 1100 in tacky gold envelopes on mine but expects a gift worth lakhs in return.'

'Kusumji has little Delhi wala taste, so get the one with the logos. Make her happy and then Ramesh will also be. You know he is a mama's boy.'

Mandy said, 'And how! Whenever I am doing anything with Ramesh – and I mean anything – his mother has to butt in. Sometimes I think she has an alarm tied to his underpants because as soon as they fall off, his mobile phone rings and it's always his mother with some urgent question that has to be answered immediately.'

I said, 'Mandy, you just have to accept that most Indian husbands come in a package of two for the price of one. Mine does as well.'

'You mean did, not does!' said my sister.

'Yes, just a slip of the tongue.'

A few minutes later, I disconnected the phone and began walking back to Shanthamaaya hurriedly. Jay was going to meet me in the woods again.

~

Raktamokshana, stated Jenna's chart for the day, which was why I was sitting next to her, holding her hand as she lay on a wooden pallet in the clinic. Officiating over the proceedings, Dr Pillai had the attendant first clean Jenna's skin with soap and water. He then gingerly applied honey on the designated sites.

The leeches were stored in a glass aquarium and Dr Pillai brought one out. 'Say hello to Krishna everyone,' he said cheerfully, as if he was introducing a newly enrolled student to the class.

As he brought the leech closer to Jenna, I could hear her whimpering. Unable to take my eyes off the repugnant creature, I watched in fascination as Krishna wiggled and then determinedly attached himself to the skin around Jenna's collarbone. Dr Pillai crooned 'Good boy' at his pet worm and then covered the creature with a piece of cotton with the same gentleness as a mother tucking a child into bed.

'Think of it as a vacuum cleaner, madam. Suck, suck, pull, pull, and all the dirt is out of your system.'

'What happens to this leech then, Dr Pillai?' I asked. 'Will it die?'

'Oh no, not to worry, we will put turmeric powder on Krishna's face and he will vomit out all the toxins.'

'Equality between species, wonderful,' I whispered to an ashen-faced Jenna. 'And here I thought they were only interested in making us humans throw up.'

Dr Pillai glared at me as he fixed a series of leeches to Jenna's skin. He attached the last one and said, 'And here finally is our little Vishnu.'

Before I could stop myself, out popped 'I guess Brahma and Mahesh didn't quite make the cut, huh?'

Jenna shut her eyes as the leeches got down to their equivalent of a Thanksgiving feast.

~

A decrepit statue. A forgotten king, with a mossy half crown. A bird fluttered towards him, perched on his head. I moved towards the window, a quick photograph with my Nikon, an allegory of life, sometimes there is a crown on your head, sometimes a crow about to defecate.

I sat by the window on the gleaming mahogany ledge, my mind filled with my acquisitions of an hour ago that I swiftly began hanging up on the museum walls of my memory.

The water was dark, a deep brown, with tiny tadpoles and minuscule black fish. My shawl, a picnic blanket, under giant two-hundred-year-old trees.

Jay sat beside me with a sleeve rolled up, a makeshift pouch. A treasure inside, one ripe mango.

'Where did you get this?' I asked him, my head on the

shawl, twigs and dead leaves crunching against my back. The aroma started my empty stomach on a rumbling song.

'I sneaked into the storeroom this morning.'

'Hello Mr Bibet! You are not supposed to go in there and you know how strict they are about following our diets! What if someone saw you?'

He mussed my hair with one hand, brought the fruit towards his face with the other, inhaled deeply, and bit the tip off.

'This is cheating, Jay.' A gurgle of laughter mixed with the sound of water as I threw a pebble into the narrow stream.

He brought the fruit up to my mouth. 'No, it's not.'

I considered him carefully as the sun dappled shadowy leaves down his arm.

'Your idea of cheating has always been different from mine,' I said, and pushed it back towards him.

I let my hand linger over his, as I clung on to a slipping resolve, trying to drown out the siren call of both gluttony and lust, two forbidden sins within the realms of this Ayurvedic world.

He was done with the mango. The peel thrown on the ground. It struck me then that a woman and a mango were similar, both fleshy fruit a minute ago, discarded shrivelled skin soon after. He bent towards me, twigs digging deeper into my back with his weight on me. His mouth was all Duke's Mangola.

An hour later, I could still taste it, smell it on my breath, mango.

Unlike Eve I didn't swallow but I had definitely sinned.

9

Bend, look beneath, be one with the ground and you shall be the possessor of the earth's darkest secrets.

Well, maybe not the earth's, but unfortunately just mine.

We were scattered around tables, a sea of faces, all dressed in white. Some of us were bent over our plantain curry and dosas, others still on rice gruel and beans cooked with grated coconut.

The uniformity of clothing gave us an anonymity, forcing us to gaze at the person within, unencumbered by subliminal prejudices.

Looking at the people at my table, I wondered, would Jenna still be smiling as gently at Lalit if she spotted him in his Sunday gear of bright T-shirts stretched over his beer belly as snugly as cling wrap?

Would I behave differently with Vivaan if I discovered that he had a penchant for floral shirts buttoned to the neck, tucked into boot-cut jeans, or worse that he only wore surfer shorts and fluorescent vests all day long?

Would Jay still bother with me, his bare toe rubbing against my leg all through dinner, under the table, if Shalini, with a waist that I could only achieve if I surgically removed half my ribcage, was sitting at this table clad in anything but this curtain of cotton?

I was too preoccupied to engage in the dinner table conversation, absorbing drifting fragments of talk and nodding absent-mindedly.

Vivaan was talking about growing cannabis on his farm. 'But then a goat ate all four plants and dropped dead on the spot!'

Javed told Anil, 'See, I told you all these things are bad for health!'

'It's not because of weed but greed,' Vivaan laughed. 'If you eat three family packs of ice cream and then get diarrhoea should I blame Baskin Robbins or your gluttony? But yes, growing it is a pain. You know, in Canada there are online suppliers like Ganja Express which are happy to drop off a box of weed at your doorstep!'

Lalit said, 'For you, the grass is definitely greener on the other side.'

Vivaan chomped on a slice of steamed beetroot and

said, 'I also think mind-altering substances are very much part of Indian culture, how else do you think the ancient rishis dreamed up all our 33 million gods if it wasn't with the help of some good old bhang?'

A puzzled Jenna asked, 'But what is this bang, Vivaan?'

'Not bang, Jenna, though it does give you a big bang for your buck! Bhang is a drink made with almonds, pistachios, rose-petal conserve, milk and cream.'

'Oh, that sounds innocuous enough.'

Vivaan laughed. 'Arrey, but the main ingredient is cannabis leaf!'

Jenna reached for her fork and inadvertently knocked her flask on to the floor. She poked her head under the tablecloth, and discovered Jay's foot over mine, and his left hand two inches away from my groin.

Shanthamaaya was very clear about its no intercourse rule, one I had continued to follow, albeit grudgingly. According to Dr Menon, though not in these exact words, an orgasm ignited the doshas like the propeller of a rocket and sent you hurtling out of the Ayurvedic orbit.

But there had been no talk of disallowing first, second and second-and-a-half bases during the treatment and I wasn't going to ask the good doctor about it either.

Jay and I, our relationship had already spun through the washing machine of lust once. All wet and slippery at the start and tumble dried at the end.

But a new chapter had begun for us, a nostalgic one, as if we were back in our early days, under star-filled skies. Jay and I dry humping on the back seat, my jeans intact though the lipstick had long been licked off.

I pushed his hand away from my thigh immediately but Jenna's face as it rose above the tablecloth was a shade paler than her kurta and I knew that she was now in on our shenanigans.

She peered in confusion around the table, taking in Jay, who was sitting between Shalini and me, with the former animatedly telling Lalit about the time she had bhang and thought birds were coming in through the window.

My ex-husband laughed, a sheepish laugh, unlike the one he had perfected in the mirror. A laugh that reminded me of other instances when I had heard it. His wife would now have to start getting used to hearing it as well.

Some part of me even wondered at that moment, was I doing this to spite her? Even the government seemed content with taking one-third of what I had, but she, the greedy bitch, had taken it all.

So it was fair then, wasn't it, this attention, time and desire that I was now siphoning out of her account, underhand, under the table?

~

Shalini entered my life on Christmas, the antithesis of Santa, though ironically she was wearing red.

That December, for an entire month, Mandira had rented a house in north Goa. It was called Casa Mila, and had a tiled roof, stained glass windows and a swimming pool flanked by papery, fuchsia pink bougainvillea.

Its three high-ceilinged bedrooms meant that, though we had to deal with the occasional spiders and lizards that brooms could not reach, there was ample space for Mandira's family, Jay and me.

I remember lots of bickering on that trip because which family can sit together for even one hour without a few Diwali crackers exploding sporadically?

'Let's go to Ashvem beach, Anshu.'

'No, Mandy. Trust me, distance does not make the heart grow fonder; it just makes people cramped in a stuffy car want to stab each other in the heart instead. Let's just go to Vagator beach, it's ten minutes away.'

'Vagator has such tacky crowds, Anshu. Don't you remember those men the last time we went there? Emerging from the water and walking straight towards us in their skimpy underwear? After generously splattering the beach with their saliva, they decided to play a game of noisy, flesh-smacking-flesh kabaddi? Please, I am not going to that beach again.'

Climbing out of the yellow tie-and-dye rope hammock, I said, 'Forget it, Mandy, you go where you want, I am going to hang by the pool. I can't argue about this any more and anyway Jay's flight gets in around noon, so I might as well wait for him.'

I dived into the pool, floating on my back, the water filling my ears and muffling all the ambient sound. Doors slamming, an engine revving up, my sister screaming for Rudra to get into the car. Sounds the water washed away till I was finally alone.

I picked up a towel and lay down on the wicker chair that flanked the pool. I was looking at the sky through a cluster of branches overhead.

'Ninety-eight beats I love you,' I said.

I cannot remember if I cried. I usually did when I thought about the baby. I fell asleep in the warm sun and I woke up two hours later, with a chequered pattern impressed on to my arm and right cheek from the chair.

Jay didn't come to Goa that day.

I got a phone call instead. 'Anshu, this Devang Mehta is hemming and hawing. I can't leave Bombay now, just a day to close the deal and I promise I will be there before Christmas Eve.'

The next day Mandira and I set off together. A family friend had asked Mandira to check up on her daughter,

Ruchi, who had abandoned the capital city for the laid-back charm of Goa six months ago.

Ruchi met us at a restaurant with a thatched roof, stained seats and multiple musical strays. Each time 'Aao huzoor tumko sitaron mein le chaloon' played on the stereo, all the dogs would begin yowling in unison.

The young girl, her bright pink hair in thin braids, didn't ask about her mother but that could also possibly be because she had food in her mouth the entire time.

She polished off three bowls of crab xacuti and mountains of French fries, but had a stomach flatter than Baba Ramdev's.

After she finished, I asked her, 'How in the world do you manage to eat like a rakshasa and still look like an apsara?'

She replied with a North Indian twang, 'I like, you know, rave.' Her racing metabolism, it turned out, was due to the fact that she danced for eight hours a night, at least four times a week.

Astounded, my sister started complimenting her for her Olympian-level dedication to fitness and asked if she took any supplements to help with her stamina. I whispered in her ear, 'It's probably drugs, you fool. And not the kind you buy at the pharmacy.'

Silenced for once in her life, Mandira focused on counting the fish bones on her plate. Mandy paid the bill, muttering under her breath, 'You tell me, Anshu, what should I report to her mother now?' Ruchi, taking the leftovers in a doggy bag, climbed on to her blue scooter and rode off with a cheery, 'I will send you all a Facebook request!'

~

The next evening I sat huddled on the porch, a mosquito repellent applied liberally on my arms and my feet which peeked out from the printed, floral kimono.

Ramesh opened the slatted door shutters, the wrought-iron chandelier overhead illuminating his balding pate. He was a stubby man with thick lips.

'Anshu, vodka? Absolut Citron! Not that Smirnoff cheap nonsense. Your favourite no, soda or tonic?' he asked.

'Just water and two cubes of ice, please.'

Jay was the vodka drinker and though I preferred wine, his irritation over wasting an entire bottle over my sole glass meant that I had started drinking vodka as well.

I gulped the drink down swiftly, wondering where my husband was. This was something I had been grappling with more and more over the past few months.

Half drunk already, I texted him, 'Love has diluted me into an evaporating brew called us.' His phone had been switched off all day.

The swimming pool had new visitors in the dark, bats that quenched their thirst with the chlorinated water. One swooped down now skimming the surface and the water rippled in answer, alive again. An image I wanted to capture and I rushed to get my camera.

The bat was gone by the time I came back but I decided to wait for another. I opened my laptop, plugged the camera cord in, deciding to use the time to free up space on the Nikon, deleting unwanted pictures. Memories encased in metal were easily erased, unlike the ones sheathed in flesh. The blue from the screen spilled on to my arms as I began browsing online while the pictures loaded, and I wandered into Facebook and accepted Ruchi's request.

We had no common friends, which was not surprising. I scrolled through her timeline, curious to see what ravers really do and halfway down the page saw a picture she had been tagged in with 'Missing all the fun Ruchi Mehra'.

I recognized him, though his face was half turned away, behind numerous unknown faces. There was a girl, clinging to him, in a red dress, with streaked hair, very young. Hell, all the people in the picture were at least a decade younger than me. All, except my husband. Merry bloody Christmas to me.

10

A pale flower tucked behind a shadowy and rather hairy ear. A streak of white captured mid-swing between the vines of a banyan tree. A black-and-white picture of a man lying on his stomach, his partner using scrabble letters to spell out a sign on his back – 'enter from backside only'. It had made me laugh so much that the first two pictures I had taken of Javed and Anil were blurred.

There were innumerable hours to fill in Shanthamaaya and we invented all kinds of silly amusements to while away our time. We sat in groups, asking each other childish questions like what movie star we resembled, and what insects. Lalit, I declared, looked like one of Dr Pillai's pet leeches. Sometimes we would sing nonsensical songs, inventing lyrics as we went along.

These were the benefits of being left to our own devices unlike always being left with our Wi-Fi-enabled devices.

Javed, at Anil's behest, had ended up sitting cross-legged on a branch, five feet above the ground, reluctantly posing for my camera. He gingerly climbed down and leaned against the trunk.

'The things I do for you!' he said as he looked at his partner, who was sprawled on the grass.

'Yes, Javed saab, now you will start with your old ghisa pita story, "I changed jobs for you, I moved cities for you!"' Anil said in his nasal voice that always held a hint of laughter.

Javed quickly interjected, 'Not just that. What about the time I had to take anti-allergy pills so your measly cat could live with us, and have you forgotten I have literally climbed mountains for you!'

Anil laughed and told me the story. 'I once forced him to come to Vaishno Devi. I didn't tell him till the last minute that my grandmother and dozens of buas and chachas were also going on the pilgrimage with us.'

I was taking candid pictures of the two as he continued, 'We stopped for tea at a dilapidated restaurant with peeling blue walls and on the television in the corner a news channel was playing live footage of the Babri Masjid demolition. My grandmother was riveted. In one hand she held the saucer that she had poured tea into, in the other she had a packet of glucose biscuits, her entire body was shaking, as she cheered, "Ramchandra ki jai!"'

A strained grimace fleeted across Javed's face, which I would not have noticed if I didn't have my camera aimed at him. The events unfolding on the television that day had left Javed reeling. He felt that it wasn't just the masjid under attack but everything he stood for. He remembered being absolutely silent in that restaurant watching the scenes of jubilation around him.

The emotions still seemed raw, even after all these years. Pushing back his curly hair, he uncrossed his legs, trying to get physically comfortable while dealing with memories that were anything but. Javed said with a bitter twist to his mouth, 'Silence is perhaps a way of life when you are both a Muslim and a homosexual in India. You get used to it, being discreet with your emotions and concealing your identity.'

No one spoke for a few minutes. Anil tried to bring the lightness back. 'But remember when we decided to come back down from Vaishno Devi on ponies? By the time we reached the bottom again, jostling and bouncing like worn-out basketballs, Javed's legs were so stiff that he could not lift them over to one side to get off the pony.'

Anil laughed, describing how he came up with a desperate solution. He placed large wooden crates on either side of the pony and coaxed his partner to stand on the crates, his trembling legs still wide apart. With Javed's weight lifted off the poor pony, Anil said, 'I yanked the animal out from between his legs like a quick diaper change.'

Looking at his partner fondly, he said, 'The things I have done for you too!'

Here was a bond that had been bludgeoned by social pressure, the law, guilt and batty relatives not to mention the added burden of religious differences. Yet it had survived, while mine with all the conventional props, including the blessings of both God and government, had self-destructed in one-third the time.

'So a perfect love story! Romeo met Romeo, and nobody died in the end!' I said, as we gathered our things and walked towards the clinic for our daily consultations.

But apparently love, straight, gay and all the rainbow colours in between, cannot exist without its conjoined twin, heartbreak.

'Nothing is perfect, darling. For a little while, Romeo here thought he was in love with a skinny and if I may add a rather manipulative Juliet,' Javed murmured, his hand firmly supporting Anil's arm.

Anil didn't reply and Javed goaded him, 'Tell her about how you defected to the other side!'

The younger man said, 'Why must you bring this up again and again? It was a long time ago.'

They say that ghee does strange things, dislodging debris not just from the body but also from the mind. A purge of both physical and emotional toxins. After a pause, Anil opened up. 'It was just a phase, a delusion is probably the right word,' he said, turning in my direction. 'She was a remarkable person, there was a certain joy she found in the mundane. She was such an optimist, not jaded and cynical like the rest of us.'

Javed chose to disagree. 'She was just an opportunist.'

'Now that I am finally talking about it, Javed, let me!'

Anil leaned towards me. 'It was her spirit I was moved by and somewhere I confused that with a physical attraction that to me, even now, seems extraordinary on my part. It was as if I had beer goggles on! You know, when you are drunk and you forget how big their hooked nose is, or how foul their breath is? In that particular moment it somehow fails to repulse you.'

'And then?' I asked.

'Then nothing,' Javed said. 'She got a flat in Indira Nagar and I got tortured for a year and a half till he finally came back to his senses.' He continued, 'Darling, love is far from perfect. It's messy, wrinkled, torn in bits and stapled together. But it is resilient or at least ours turned out to be.'

The path narrowed near the pond. Javed slowed down, gallantly waving me ahead.

I looked at the flower in his buttonhole. A rose today, the traditional symbol of love. But love, I thought, was better symbolized by the Himalayan balsam, which I had seen near Shimla many years ago. A wild weed once rooted nearly impossible to eradicate, the fuchsia flowers impervious to poison.

We took another picture that day. When patients were purged and finally released, bag in hand, back in their everyday attire, all the residents, doctors and therapists posed with them for a group photograph on the sprawling entrance staircase.

Pam and Glenda were leaving before their twenty-one days were over. Even the doyens of Shanthamaaya had to bow before their marketing departments. Celebrities, writers, bloggers, people who could spur the Ayurveda retreat to greater glory, were given concessions unlike the rest of us.

Madhu was talking to me but I wasn't really listening. I was watching Jenna, who was standing beside Lalit. His hand was on her shoulder and she was listening to him talking animatedly.

The polite smile on her face jarred with the matter-of-fact way she was trying to peel his fingers off her. Jenna's eyes were fixed on his face, as if she felt that if she kept nodding agreeably with whatever he was saying, he would not notice her gesture.

The last two days, Jenna had been watching me too, her eyes full of questions but how could I explain to her something which I barely understood myself.

My sister had called again that afternoon to talk about Jay.

'Anshu, for God's sake, what's the point of this stubbornness to stay there. It's like a recovering alcoholic deciding to open a bar.'

I had never been an alcoholic, but after we separated, I did exchange one addiction for another. I figured if love was nothing but a play of chemicals in the brain, then perhaps I could replace a man with a pill, or a bunch of pills in this case.

It worked for a while. But then I was unable to stop. The day I cut back on the pills, my anxiety would come rushing back. I was unable to fall asleep, even the sound of swallowing my own saliva would wake me up.

Grief, a black hole, the gravity of loss so strong, even light that entered could not escape.

It was Mandira who left her husband, her son and even her eight-month-old baby and came to Bombay to help me. She took all the scattered pieces of my fragmenting mind and coaxed them back together. She dragged me to a psychiatrist, an acupuncturist and even a faith healer, who knocked me on the head with his broom to drive evil spirits away. But fundamentally, she helped me recover, just by being there for me.

'Anshu, Vivaan, we must stay in touch!'

Pam enveloped us in a bear hug and said goodbye cheerfully. She emailed me a copy of that picture eventually. Fifteen people spread over three wide steps.

Jay stood with Shalini, her head leaning against his arm. Madhu and Babaji peeped over Anil's shoulder, Javed by his side. Dr Menon was beaming in the middle with the other doctors. Vyacheslav and Afanasy stood next to Lalit, who had a grin on his face and his hand on Jenna's head as if she was his prized Siamese kitten. And Vivaan, who towered over everyone else, was standing beside me, as I gazed to the left distractedly. We never took another group picture.

11

An elaborate arrangement of hand signals began to pass between Jay and me, as if we were basketball players on a court, indicating to each other to move right and left without the other team knowing.

Elbows on the table, tapping fingers together meant he could get away soon. Rubbing his forehead, casually, as we crossed each other in the clinic corridors, his young wife beside him, meant plans had changed.

Half an hour snatched when she was in the steam room. An hour when he was meant to be practising meditation.

'I was smoking near the yoga pavilion,' he would tell his wife or, 'I was walking on the left end of the estate.' Fourteen acres was a lot of space to get lost in.

We met in a half-demolished stone turret sometimes, the remnants of the old palace's boundary walls. We would sit on its stone stairs, pull down a branch of a mulberry tree, filled with red fruit slowly turning to a purple bruised ripeness. He would pick a few ripe mulberries, relishing the tart fruit, while I soaked in the nostalgia that being with each other evoked.

On one of our walks, we stumbled upon a forgotten temple, a tattered red cloth around a small idol, a mossy granite plaque with inscriptions and in the corner a larger wooden statue of Shiva covered with an old and battered plastic sheet keeping vigil.

'Isn't it strange that God, love, time are all invisible, and yet they define our entire existence,' I said to Jay as we walked back, now hurrying because his wife would have just about finished her massage and skin rejuvenating treatments.

One afternoon after he had a brutal colonic, we met at the Prince, in this instance unexpectedly.

I was sitting alone, going through my emails. Disgruntled, he sat across the table smoking, his face gloomy. 'Your friends Anil and Javed must be enjoying this up the ass business but I think it is disgusting.'

'Stop being mean, Jay. I am very fond of them.'

I touched his cheek tenderly. 'Do the course properly, stop smoking and it will really help you.'

He shook his head, taking another long drag, breathing toxins gleefully into his lungs.

'While I am here, I am doing it, but in the long run this Ayurveda business is not for me. The only reason I came back here was because of Lalit. He was the one going on about finding an Ayurvedic cure for his gout.'

My first instinct had been right. My ex-husband felt that away from Lalit's other cronies, bereft of distractions, he had a better chance of sweet-talking his cousin and closing a deal with him.

'I am fifty-two, Anshu. I am tired of running around, convincing people to invest in this fund over that, arguing over 7 per cent and 8.5 per cent returns when the big money goes to the big bosses of the fund house. I have been after Lalit to throw out that useless Chatterjee and let me handle his investments. Once that happens, I don't have to hustle for other people any more, Anshu.'

He seemed to have it all planned out. 'I already have a few smaller clients who will shift with me. Once Lalit is on board, I can finally start my own company. I have the papers here but the fucker is really making me run around instead of signing on the dotted line and getting it over with.'

'And in return you are willing to be his flunkey, Jay?'

'Big deal, Anshu. So I will have to laugh at his stupid remarks and get him hookers every once in a while, so be it. And now, Anshu, don't start nagging me about this or my smoking,' he said, with a broad smile. 'You are not my wife any more.'

He finished his cigarette, grinding the butt under his foot.

I opened my jhola, pulled out a tissue. 'I think you need this?' I said. An old ritual of ours, one that Jay seemed to remember equally well, because he looked at me sheepishly. He picked up the butt, wrapped it in tissue and then leaning forward dropped it in my bag.

'You throw it, Anshu! It's been years since you last cleaned up my mess.'

Once, eager to please him, I would have accepted his trash but I handed it back to him.

'I think you should do it yourself.' He accepted it. His voice held a note of amusement. 'I guess I have to start training Biwi No. 2 to do it now.'

~

I crossed her on the stairs the next day. Her frizzy hair was pinned, two twists on either side secured with gold clips. Our arms brushed against each other. It was an odd feeling to want to be exactly like someone else, to want her skin, her waist, her youth and yet dislike her enough to imagine, just for a moment, pushing her down the stairs.

Around her, I always felt bigger, clumsier, less appealing. Why would he want me when he could have her and her perkier breasts?

'They are implants!' He grinned when I asked him later, a flippant tone masking my insecurities. We were sitting in the woods. He had come bearing more gifts of fruits. Three pears from the storeroom this time.

'Hard but springy, you know what I mean, like two trampolines bang in the middle of her chest,' he said, making me giggle.

'Stop it, Jay.'

'And the nose is not real either. The first surgery went wrong and for her second rhinoplasty I refused to go to the hospital to meet her. She was livid, but couldn't say anything as I was paying through my nose for her new one.'

Jay made me laugh, he always had. He had also always taken advantage of the fact, like he was doing right now, his hand sliding from my foot, gliding up my leg under the white cotton.

'Jay, my legs are not shaved,' I blurted out, the first thing that came to my mind, trying to push his hand away.

'Nor is anything else, as I have seen with my own eyes!' He laughed, watching me squirm. 'But who is worried about hair? Right now, Juju, I don't care if you have cactus sprouting on your thighs, as long as I can get between your legs.'

'It's a commendable mission, Bibet. After all, they do say that heaven lies between a woman's legs, don't they?'

'If that is heaven, Juju, then even better. Remember Prince Charles saying he wished to be reborn as a tampon? Add me to that list so that I can also stay in heaven forever!'

'Doesn't sound very hygienic,' I said with what I am sure was a silly grin plastered across my face. 'You will be replaced quickly, tampons have to be changed frequently, otherwise bacteria gets into your bloodstream.'

'Just shut up, Anshu.'

And I did, but I refused to part my pyjama-clad legs.

The next evening, under the dome-shaped porch, with a board of backgammon as our alibi, it was a different story. He was appreciative about his young wife.

'She is like a child really, doesn't mean anything she says! Look, even this place, she was grumbling about it, was forcing us to leave and yesterday after I showed her that it has been featured in *Harper's Bazaar* and *Vogue*, the actual American editions not our desi ones, she is busy sending her friends links to the articles and posting a thousand pictures.'

He said she looked up to him, was always deferring to his opinion, she boosted his confidence.

Rolling the dice, a six and a four, I knocked off two of his round, white discs from the board.

'I should learn from her,' I said, 'about always massaging a man's ego, as much as his penis.'

Though when I looked back, in the early days hadn't I done the same thing, albeit unconsciously. He, the sophisticated man showing me the world, while I looked at it, and at him, in wide-eyed gratitude.

'You are not massaging anything right now, Juju, and I am still here.'

And there was the main course, the filet mignon, that I wanted to dissect. 'Yes, Jay, tell me, why are you here with me?'

Before he could say anything, answers like we were on *Kaun Banega Crorepati* began popping in my mind.

A: Nostalgia. B: I was bored and you happened to be here. C: Regret. D: A song, 'When a Man Loves a Woman', the Michael Bolton version circa 1991.

But he didn't answer my question. A shake of his head, an ambiguous shrug, was all he could offer.

Another roll of the dice, and the game continued.

12

There was a worn noticeboard in the high-ceilinged library. On it were pinned carefully laminated articles advertising Shanthamaaya's charms and notices about upcoming events.

A misspelled circular announced an Ayurveda cooking class at 3 p.m. at fifteen hundred rupees per head. Jenna, Anil and Madhu had already signed their names up for the class. There were still two slots vacant. I wrote my name down and then immediately scratched it out. I preferred keeping my afternoons free in case Jay was able to get away.

I picked up a worn copy of *The Catcher in the Rye* and moved to a table under the slow-moving fan by the window. The rain outside was drowning out all other sounds when Lalit swaggered into the library, stood idly by the door for a few moments and then plonked himself on the chair beside mine.

He took the book from my hand, peered at the simple cream jacket with its orange border.

'Looking at this cover itself would put me to sleep.'

He had a peculiar way of speaking, a condescending sneer, like his wealth also made him the arbiter of good taste and all fine things.

At restaurants, I had seen him placing his lunch order – the chef would be summoned, something special off the menu would always have to be made just for him, the most expensive wine had to be ordered. And God forbid, if the hapless server dropped a tiny bit of cork inside the wine bottle. The microscopic particle was treated like a fleck of uranium and the now radioactive rosé along with the hapless sommelier would be summarily banished to an underground bunker never to be seen again.

I tried to keep my annoyance at bay.

'Haven't you heard, don't judge a book by its cover, Lalit? It's a classic and meant to be very good.'

He placed the book on the table and pushed it back towards me smugly, saying, 'Yaar, same thing I have been telling you, Anshu! Judge me also under the covers, I am meant to be very good too!'

As Jay's wife I had been obliged to politely sit through

countless dinners with him, where he would ply me with his innuendoes while I brushed them off.

I was under no such obligation now.

'Lalit, sorry, but I don't find this kind of talk appealing in any way.'

Lalit leaned forward. 'Achha, not my jokes but you still seem to find my cousin very appealing, right?'

He waited for a reply and when none was forthcoming, he said, 'What did you think, Anshu, he won't tell me what you two are up to?'

Revulsion, like a physical force, made me stand up and push away from the table.

Lalit caught my arm. 'Sit, Anshu, what's the big deal, yaar, we have all gone back to take second helpings of our favourite dessert. This is the same thing.'

I wanted to find Jay. I was finding it hard to think of a single reason why he would tell his cousin about us.

'Sit,' he repeated. 'Don't worry, I won't tell anyone. I know you like to keep things to yourself.' He laughed. 'Even Jenna doesn't know, right? Don't worry, I won't tell her. Now, that is a rasgulla I wouldn't mind trying a bite of.'

Lalit continued talking and I was reminded of my favourite cartoon, which I used to watch in my grandmother's house. My hair in two oiled pigtails, sitting on the floor, *Jungle Book* playing on the bulky television.

The green snake, his eyes glowing, growing larger, black circles swirling in the middle. I couldn't remember his name and then it came to me, Kaa, yes, Lalit reminded me of Kaa as he tried to suck me into his odious world.

He had invited Jenna to his farmhouse but she had not yet accepted his invitation. 'If you also come, Anshu, she will agree for sure. Don't worry, I will invite Jay also so you both can continue this . . .' He left it unfinished, eyebrows raised. 'Whatever you both are calling it.'

I did not know if in the world outside these gates I would have anything in common with Jenna. If our dinner party conversation would go beyond the polite 'nice to meet you'.

But getting to know her in Shanthamaaya, her kindness, her endearing eccentricities, her naive view of colourful, cultural India, I felt fiercely protective of my young friend.

'Leave her alone, Lalit, she isn't even your type.'

All the women I had seen Lalit parade over the years looked as if they had been picked from the same catalogue – pneumatic lips and breasts to match. They were all the exact opposite of Jenna, with her frail frame and cropped hair.

'Like the food, other choices are also limited here, Anshu.'

He leaned back in his chair and with a cynical laugh he said, 'They say beauty is in the eye of the beholder, but I say that a beauty is whoever lets you hold her.'

~

A stairway, a painted ceiling, a woman walking by in a cream sari, all were dimly illuminated by the sunlight spilling over from a courtyard.

I passed a small alcove with wooden pillars and an urli with floating red hibiscus flowers, part of a shrine to a long-deceased queen.

My stomach was burning. Heartburn and a hot temper are both primary pitta characteristics.

I hurried on, my feet slapping loudly on the tiled walkway, till I finally found Jay.

He was sitting inside Kesava's small office near the performance dais. The yoga teacher had a printed list in his hand and was going over it with my ex-husband.

I entered the office and pulled Jay by his sleeve. 'I want to talk to you right now.' My words came out louder and sharper than I had intended, echoing in the arches and domes along the corridor.

Kesava looked at us mutely. He had seen us as a couple when we had come together but of course he wouldn't remember. Shanthamaaya was a carnival. People were constantly climbing on to the carousel, getting off and going their way. It would be difficult for the employees to keep track of who came when and with whom in the past.

But he was sensible enough to stand up. 'Please, Anshu madam, take a seat. It is time for my tea break anyway.' I shut the door after him.

'How could you go and tell your vile cousin about us? Is that one more way of trying to bond with him, laughing together at my expense with, "Oh that poor Anshu, see how she still has the hots for me?"'

'Anshu, I swear I don't know what you are talking about.'

'Don't lie to me, Jay.'

'I swear, I am not. At least tell me what happened.'

When I finished telling him about my encounter in the library with Lalit, he said, 'He played you. All he had was a hunch. He tied it to a line, threw it in your direction and you took the bait. Now Lalit knows about us but it's thanks to you and not me. What kind of a man do you think I am, Anshu? How could you believe that I would let you down like that?'

'Because you have, many times before, Jay.'

'Really, Anshu, was it all me? Do you know how inadequate you had started making me feel?'

Inadequate was an adjective I would have used for myself in the past. Jay with his Columbia degree gleamed with the patina of old money, though it was all hanging up on walls or dotting the shelves of his home. His grandfather had given the bulk of his money to his only son, Lalit's father, while he had given his youngest daughter, my imperious mother-in-law, extravagant gifts all through her life. Antiques and pieces of silver, jewellery and expensive art, along with an Ivy League education for his grandson.

I had never met anyone like Jay, a man so well travelled, worldly. My mother had been equally impressed. After we got engaged, she went around boasting to our various relatives about what she considered one of her future son-in-law's most admirable traits – 'He doesn't look at all Indian, looks like a proper foreigner.'

She once told me that if it had been an arranged match, it would have never gone past the first meeting. I would have been summarily rejected because I was darker than the prospective groom.

Jay's skin was four shades paler than mine.

Casper the friendly ghost was another name I used to call him by, especially to needle him, when he spent hours in the sun, boiled to a bright red, his skin peeling off in strips for the next few days. He, in turn, would tease me, putting his arm next to mine in the sunlight, and say, 'Look, black-and-white stripes, you know who our baby will resemble the most, a zebra!'

A baby. Five years after we were married, a week after our anniversary in fact, I finally went to the gynaecologist.

A battery of tests and I got the results, my eggs were as good as a twenty-one-year-old's.

'I think we should get your husband tested, Mrs Lulla,' the sympathetic doctor said softly.

Implied in his tone was his weary experience of how this played out. Very few men are open to getting their sperm tested. After all, if a couple is infertile then isn't it always a woman's fault? Barren, a bleak word for both land and women. In Hindi, we have a word for it, 'baanjh', an infertile woman. I had never heard its male equivalent.

If Jay was reluctant, he didn't let on. It was a game at first. 'Come on,' I said, 'this is a chance to relive your youth, go pretend you are a teenager, jerk off and fill this specimen jar.'

'Nope, I am an adult now, I have a wife. Come on, Juju, do your job.' Unfortunately Jay didn't manage to competently do the only job that I had actually left to his hands, seal the specimen jar tightly. Because on the way to the gynaecologist it spilled in the bag.

Round two was not as much fun and nor were the results. His little soldiers were in dire need of a compass, it seemed. They would set out to conquer the northern territories, get disoriented, spin around and head back the way they came.

'The chances of pregnancy in these circumstances are very low, Mrs Lulla,' I was told.

So I bowed down to the odds and a year later, much to my surprise, I beat them.

Two pink lines on three home pregnancy tests meant I was undoubtedly pregnant.

Over a dinner where I had clearly not made the mulligatawny soup up to her exacting standards, Jay relayed the news to his mother. She, of course, immediately took the credit.

'See, Jay, I told you we must listen to the Vaastu lady. Her suggestion to paint our kitchen red because it will increase the fertility quotient in the house was right! Thank heavens, I convinced your wife to do it because it has clearly worked!'

After dinner, we went for a walk around the building. It was warm, my floral shirt stuck clammily to my arms. 'Jay, you know it's not because of that crazy bat!'

'I am just grateful that something worked, Anshu, and by the way don't call my mother a bat, the crazy part I really can't refute.'

'No! I meant the Vaastu lady is a crazy bat not your mother, I would never say that.' Though to be honest what I meant was that I would never say that to him.

'I know, I was just pulling your leg, Juju,' he said, a dent appearing in his right cheek as he smiled.

'I wonder if the baby will also have your dimple.'

Jay said it was unlikely. He didn't have one till he was eight and now realized he had probably developed it because of a childhood penchant for constantly sucking on kala khatta golas.

I first thought he was making it up. But it turned out to be an actual phenomenon – scientists called it popsicle panniculitis.

He put his hand on my shoulder. This was a new development. Ever since he had found I was pregnant, he had begun draping his arm around me. It reminded me of the way I used butter paper to wrap sandwiches, gentle, yielding, careful.

We walked three more rounds of the bare compound with a handful of straggly trees near the boundary wall. We were silent, amid the sounds of shrieking horns and snatches of a song blaring from Mr Gandhi's ground-floor apartment when we passed his living room window.

I could see us retracing the same path time and again in the years to come. A pram at first and then holding on to a little girl's hand, one who had her father's beautiful grey eyes and a gola in her mouth.

I had booked an appointment for an early sonography at Tulip Nursing Centre. Jay was also supposed to come, but an irate client meant that he had to rush to Marine Lines.

The radiologist, Dr Batra, a middle-aged man with the flushed face of a heavy drinker, asked, 'I hope you have had enough water.'

I nodded. 'Three glasses of water and then no going to the bathroom as the receptionist had instructed. In fact, it is rather uncomfortable.'

He shrugged. 'Get used to it. My wife says pregnancy is a great equalizer. It's a condition where your stomach and breasts grow while your brain and bladder shrink.' He laughed uproariously at his own joke before putting the probe on my stomach.

I had a clown for a radiologist, I thought – he even had a bona fide red nose.

'See, that is the gestation sac and that inside it is the yolk sac that provides nutrition to the growing embryo. Congratulations, you are seven weeks pregnant. Hang on, let me see if we can get the heartbeat as well.' He moved the ultrasound probe carefully on my stomach.

'Ahh, there it is, embryo cardiac activity, 98 beats a minute.'

'Is that normal?'

'Yes, don't worry, the range at this stage of pregnancy is from 100 to 120 bpm, but these are just guidelines.'

As he was mapping measurements on the screen he

looked at me with a smile and sang, 'Do dil mile rahe hain magar chupke chupke.'

I knew that song, it was from an old Bollywood movie, and when I looked at him perplexed, he said, 'Two hearts, meeting each other secretly, isn't that what is happening within you now?'

In an instant, he had flipped both a corny song and my perception of him upside down. Two hearts. I could sense mine, 60, 70 beats a minute, but there was another, smaller, faster, harder at work inside me.

On the way home, sitting in the back seat of the blue Honda, the reports in a plastic bag next to me, I gently rubbed my stomach. Ninety-eight was an odd name for a baby, but it was what I started calling my little one from then on. My miracle baby.

'You know something, I am scared,' I said to Jay as he fetched me from Harmony. I had joined the playschool as an assistant teacher fourteen months ago and so far my job entailed entertaining more than educating largely incontinent three-year-olds.

We were heading to Tulip Nursing Centre for the next scan at sixteen weeks. Jay had been late and now we were stuck in traffic because of a stalled rickshaw.

'It's such a cruel world, you see it everywhere. You read in the papers today about that Bunsha case? That little girl, her father bought her a cycle for her birthday. She was thrilled with her present, riding it round and round the park, when a coconut fell on her head and she died on the spot.'

'What is with all this morbid talk, Juju? I think your hormones are playing havoc with your mind.' He smiled. 'And your weight as well. By the way, how much have you gained already? Nine, ten pounds. All this "I am craving for peanut chikki but only the kind you get at Bharat Stores!" is adding up, I tell you.'

After a short wait in the dreary reception, we were ushered inside.

'Let's see, is your bladder half empty or half full?' said Dr Batra jocularly.

He moved the probe slightly lower and I saw the baby on the screen, a small head, tiny hands and legs.

Jay was standing by the examination bed, peering at the screen, holding my hand gently.

'Let me take the crown to rump measurements of the fetus and then we will figure out whose nose the baby has – yours or your mother-in-law's.'

He moved the probe and paused. I felt the cold, sticky metal lift away from my skin.

Dr Batra glanced at me and then looked away. He picked up his probe once again and placed it on my stomach.

'There is no heartbeat, the fetus is showing a growth

of fifteen weeks. I am so sorry but the heart must have stopped sometime last week.'

There was a sound in my ears, a high-pitched hum, that blocked out everything else. I remember sitting in that small examination room, among posters that stated 'Paediatric Imaging and Sex Determination Is Illegal'. Sitting with my husband silently, tears rolling down both our faces.

Jay called the gynaecologist. We did not know what the next steps were, where to go, what to do.

I was not listening to their conversation, I could only hear the loop playing repeatedly in my head.

Ninety-eight beats and no more, I thought. The single sentence running round and round in my head till I was in the centre of a whirlwind.

That night I lay in bed with my dead child inside me. Staring at the ceiling. Looking at nothing.

I remember not sleeping. I remember waiting to go to the hospital in the morning to deliver a corpse.

They called what had happened to me a missed miscarriage where the cervix remains closed though the baby has passed away. The heart must not have developed correctly – chromosomal abnormality – they would send the remains for testing. Words and more words that didn't matter.

In the weeks to come, our families muttered platitudes filled with 'next time' or 'try again'.

I would nod my head though I wanted to scream that my baby was not a fused light bulb that could just be replaced with another.

Jay kept repeating that we should be grateful, we had each other, a good life.

Yes, grateful that life didn't ask for its full pound of flesh. There wasn't even a pound to take, was there? Just mere grams of tissue and tiny bones that meant the world to me.

A cycle began at my insistence, one that rotated around modern fertility rituals like ovulation dates, vaginal scans and a totem of sex without pleasure as a lucky charm. It didn't work.

'Come early from work, we have to do it today,' I texted him looking at my ovulation chart.

That evening, when I rushed back from Harmony, he was already home. A three-year-old had thrown up on my shirt, the smell of vomit still in my hair, but nothing mattered beyond getting his sperm to reach my fertile eggs before they boiled over and we lost the narrow window.

He could not perform, not that day or the next, not even with graphic images of porn, an orgy of naked limbs spread open on our bedroom television.

A few months of repeated failures and finally I said the obvious.

'We need to find a sperm donor.'

His eyes were like a calm sea and then I saw a churning beneath, a low tide, as he withdrew into himself, away from me.

I didn't see it then, I only realized this much later, looking into the crystal ball of hindsight, the only one that offers clarity about the past.

Standing in Kesava's dusty office, my nose leaking, I said, 'I lost a child and then I lost you.'

He held me, his hand stroking my hair.

The outside world began intruding. I could hear Kesava and Shalini in the corridor. The acoustics of the old palace, designed to amplify ceremonial sounds, brought their footsteps and their voices closer and closer to us. He moved away from me just before the door opened.

His wife stood at the threshold.

'I've been looking for you, Jay. What are you doing here?'

Jay blinked a few times and then said smoothly, 'Shalini, nothing. Anshu came looking for me. I was sitting here getting a yoga chart for Lalit, you can ask Kesava. She started crying. I was just explaining to her that she should leave the past behind, move on, we all have.'

Shalini looked at me, confident in her youth, her

beauty, her husband's sincerity. Looked at me like I was nothing at all, a beggar woman who had been knocking on their rolled-up car windows. She shook her head slightly and said, 'How can you still keep chasing him? It's so desperate!'

13

My camera was filling up with pictures of tomatoes, green and red, battered and oozing, that had fallen on the ground because of the rain.

Wanting solitude, I had once again picked up my breakfast apple and headed down to the vegetable garden.

I was filled with humiliation. He had lied. He had reduced me to a hysterical, pathetic creature in front of her, in front of Shalini, and I had not said a word.

I had not been able to sleep all night, going over and over the confrontation in Kesava's room. I felt reduced, belittled. Even this tomato plant had more dignity than me, I thought.

I touched the leaves, bending down to take in a lungful of the green fragrance. It had a purpose at least. It was here to give out oxygen, grow tiny yellow flowers that changed to icy-green fruit and then turned an orangey red like a blazing sunset. It had vines reaching out to places unexplored, to grow upward with a vertical support, or spread over land. Wider if not higher, for who is to say which direction is more worthwhile, soaring through the air or staying low, covering more ground?

I was taking another picture when Vivaan came by.

He thrust his face in front of my lens.

'I also want to be a tomato,' he laughed, 'because you seem to be so fascinated by them.'

I had wanted to be alone, but his smile, the warmth in his tone, made me happy. I thought his company would do me some good.

'Come, sit here, let me take a few pictures of you as well.'

The lack of sleep was evident in my flat voice and in the rings under my eyes.

I asked him to sit still as I took a burst of pictures. Cropped portraits of his face, of his eyes, a pale tinge to the white sclera like the turmeric-infused milk Mummy used to make us drink when we were running a fever.

Jay, Shalini and Lalit were walking down the stairs towards the clinic. Vivaan waved out at them but I just turned my face away, pretending not to have seen them.

Vivaan turned back towards me and began making goofy faces, moving closer and closer as I kept adjusting the focus till his nose was touching the camera lens. When I brought the camera down, his face was less than an inch away from mine.

He pulled out his phone from his jhola and said, 'I wrote this yesterday. See if you like it.'

He began reading aloud from the small screen, 'Come sit beside me in this fragrant breeze and we will travel to places we have never seen, to frangipani-lined streets and to purple lavender fields, things we had seen once in a dream.'

'Vivaan, you are a poet? You know poetry is primarily a vata trait? How many have you written?' I asked.

Solemnly he took my hand. 'Promise me you will not steal my poems. I want to publish a book some day.'

'Of course, Vivaan. Don't be crazy,' I said and he laughed.

'Some hack at Lintas sent me this baloney to be used for our advertising brochure! I knew you would be impressed, you are such a dodo, going, "Oh, you are a poet, the next Gulzar!"'

I smiled despite all my fatigue. 'You ass! Can't believe I fell for that!'

A brief pause as he gazed at me and, when he had completed this odd examination, he said, 'Keep falling, na, Anshu, I've been falling all over you.' He paused. 'But only in yoga class.'

'Vivaan, you are such a flirt. I have seen you even trying to charm the pants off Madhu, for God's sake.'

'Just trying to make as many people happy in as short a time, Anshu,' he grinned.

'Stop this rubbish, I bet you are going to outlive me for sure,' I said sharply, though deep inside I knew that cancer was a nostalgic beast with a penchant for returning to the neighbourhoods where it once lived.

~

That night Jay turned up once again outside my room.

I wanted to leave him there. Close the door. Go back to bed.

But he put his hand on my cheek and said, 'Sorry, Juju, you tell me what else could I have said? How does it matter what she thinks anyway?'

A nonchalant shrug, a smile, his voice coaxing. 'You are making a big deal of trivial matters as usual. If I tell her the truth, do you think she would let me stay here for even a day longer? I had to make up something on the spot, I didn't know what else to say and I only did it because I want to stay here, Juju – with you.'

I did have a tendency to overreact or at least that's what Jay had often said over the years.

He walked in, pulling me towards the bed till I was lying down with him. His nose was buried in my neck.

'You smell different today, something sweet, like jaggery?' It was honey, part of a skin rejuvenating treatment and a relief from the medicated sesame oil which was reminiscent of nothing else but old socks.

'I saw you this morning taking pictures of Vivaan. You haven't taken even one of me, Juju.'

There was a hint of annoyance underneath his teasing tone.

'I can't ask you to pose for me, can I? Or what will your wife think? That I am now running behind you with my camera as well!'

A sudden realization crossed my mind.

'Jay, won't your wife get up and wonder where you are?'

'No, she won't.'

'How do you know?' I asked, curious, yet dreading the answer.

He was silent and then that staccato laugh. 'Don't worry, she won't. I crushed two Somapure pills into her glass of vata water.'

'What is that?'

'Sleeping pills, and chill, Juju, they are the herbal kind so I am sure it will have your sanction.'

'That's not right, Jay. How can you do something like that?'

I sat up, the room was dark, the only light coming in was from under the bathroom door. He pulled me back down.

'It's perfectly safe, Anshu. I use it myself if I haven't slept well for a few days or when I am jet-lagged. So all that will happen is that she will sleep better than she has in a long while, big deal!'

'That's not the point, Jay, you just can't give someone pills without their knowledge.'

He stopped stroking my hair, his tone petulant. 'Enough, Anshu, don't spoil this now! What was I supposed to do otherwise? How could I get away? You want me to stop coming here, I will.'

His voice was flat, cold. I knew that tone.

I remembered the times he would get upset, withdraw, the days of silence, my attempts to appease him, repeatedly apologizing, only to be met with a wall of coldness.

'That's not what I meant, I don't want you to go, Jay.' I shook my head, holding him tight.

My answer seemed to placate him. He lay down beside me and soon his hands reached under my kurta, touching my breasts. His eyes were dark, the grey just a rim.

After a few minutes, he started pushing against me.

'Shit,' he said, 'I am going to get bloody blue balls like

this. Come on, Juju, we can't keep behaving like we are in high school!'

'Don't, Jay. You know what Dr Menon says.'

'Fuck him. I want to, don't you?' he asked.

'Let's wait, Bibet, just a few more days.'

He turned away from me, the irritation evident in his voice. 'You know, you are right, it's better I go. I don't know why I came here in the first place. Don't worry, I won't bother you again.'

He began walking towards the door, setting a flurry of panic within me once again. I thought I had eradicated this woman, this needy, clingy creature, but she had merely been in exile, waiting to reclaim her place. I rushed to him, caught his arm. 'No, don't go,' I said, 'please.'

He didn't say a word. I could feel his hands on my pyjamas, rough hands, struggling with the drawstring till he undid the knot. They fell to the floor, followed by my plain underwear, both pooling around my feet.

We had sex. Sit, lie down, roll over, come – a gamut of old tricks that felt brand new.

'I want you, Jay,' I said repeatedly that night.

Only much later would I realize that want is a bin liner. It accepts scraps willingly.

~

The elephants were standing in front of the temple by the lake. Gold, red and green panels adorned their heads though they had chains around their hind legs, looped around their backs and stomachs. They were eating shrubs and defecating all over the garden. A mahout hit their front legs with a stick to get them to stand in a straight line.

There were a handful of bare-chested, mundu-clad priests and a parade of boys carrying flags: the sound of drums and cymbals ringing through the air. The procession would visit various temples in the area today.

All the Shanthamaaya residents were huddled together on the grass. I was sitting with Anil, laughing at his jokes, though my attention was on Jay. He was standing a few feet away and, despite the heat, his kurta was buttoned right to the top.

The previous night, I had seen two hickeys, dark welts on his shoulder as he switched the lamp on. He was looking for his underwear, he had to leave quickly. I didn't point them out to him.

The tawdry discussion on what to say, how to conceal them – I didn't want the night to end in that manner.

'It's nothing, just a bruise, the squash ball hit me. You know that Vijay is a rotten player, I wanted to smash the racket on his head,' he had said to me about a similar mark many years ago.

Shalini had slept with my husband then. And now I had slept with hers.

The only guilt I felt was that my treatment had been sidetracked. Two orgasms, one with his tongue and one sitting on top with his penis deep inside, had probably sent my doshas hurtling like flaming comets and now no amount of massages could guide them back into a stable orbit.

Shalini glanced in my direction, her face slightly puffier than usual. She seemed grumpy and was standing sullenly next to him.

Marriage can turn into a sharp blade that slices through desire like it's a dead fish, the head swiftly severed, the flesh picked clean, till all that's left are the unwanted bones. Perhaps that's what had happened to theirs, just as it had happened to mine.

I could see my ex-husband's nose turning red in the sun, his cheeks flushing. He should go and stand in the shade, I thought.

I knew this man. I knew his weaknesses, from his fragile skin to his other frailties. His friends, the many that surrounded him, had laughingly told me that he was not reliable when we had got engaged. He would effusively promise to be there for their birthdays and anniversaries, animatedly discussing who was the best bartender to hire, promising to get a well-known DJ's number, and then often just not show up.

But he had this way of focusing his attention on someone, noticing the smallest details about a person, attributes that no one had recognized before, and he would inevitably manage to charm their disgruntlements away. Jay had always managed to make people feel alive. It was this quality that had made me fall deeply in love with him all those years ago.

Love. But what is love except giving pieces of ourselves to another? And what happens to those bits after it's over? It's not a loan that can be returned, nor like a chameleon's tail does the jagged nub just grow back.

I had given him too many pieces of me, I had been left with too many hollow parts. I did not know if I could fill all of them myself, if I could be whole again, without him.

~

During my daily consultation the next morning, I sat across from Dr Menon like a truant student summoned to the headmaster's office.

He had started, in his usual convivial manner, telling me not to go back to eating spices on my return to the real world. 'There should be just enough chilli in the food to come out and say hello, not embrace you and all your ancestors all the way till 1892.'

But after he took my pulse, his expression became more sombre and he began interrogating me.

'There is an imbalance again, Anshu. I don't understand. What can be causing it? Is it because of Jay? I don't think you are really all right despite what you say.'

'I don't care what anyone thinks!' I said sharply.

Dr Menon didn't lose his composure. He kept looking at me with his kind eyes, and I immediately apologized.

'I understand that this is a difficult situation for you. But you are here to balance your doshas, to find equilibrium, peace. When you come here we ask you to leave all your problems behind. But this situation can't be helped now.'

He shifted in his chair, waited for a few moments, all traces of his usual joviality absent.

'I spoke to Shalini and Jay yesterday, their friend had also come for the meeting.'

'His cousin,' I said, more to fill the silence than to correct Dr Menon.

'I asked them if they would prefer to leave because Shalini has been complaining almost daily that she is very dissatisfied by my treatment.'

A sinking feeling in my stomach. 'And they agreed?'

He ignored my question and continued, 'She couldn't tolerate the ghee she said and even after purgation she has not been feeling better. Has been suffering from migraines.'

I did not want to hear the intimate details of Shalini's health.

'What did Jay say? Did he say they are leaving?'

'It would be better if he did leave, especially for you, Anshu.'

14

My sister said she had been trying to call me all afternoon. Sometimes I wondered if it was not worry but guilt that drove her to check on me incessantly. Her life had always been a well-tarred highway with signposts while mine was a convoluted path that I had to try to hack through a jungle.

She was thinner, richer, happier and, I have often suspected, our mother's favourite. But what I envied the most was that she had children.

'Thanks to him, I have been cracking up all day.'

She was talking about my nephew, Rudra, who had apparently created havoc by teaching both his grandmothers to make WhatsApp video calls.

'His Dadi is still unable to differentiate between an audio and a video call. This morning, she swung open the bathroom door and passed the phone to my father-in-law while he was reaching for a towel and said, "Mohanji, take this, Mandira's mother is calling from Bombay to wish you happy birthday!" At which point Mummy promptly hung up as she had had more than her fill of seeing Mohanji in his wrinkled birthday suit.'

Imagining Mummy's face at what would have been a grisly sight had me in splits as well.

'You seem to be in a great mood today!' my sister said.

'It's part of the detox, Mandy. They cleanse you of all toxins – meat, caffeine, sugar – and stuff happiness in its place or maybe it's just the effects of that pill that Dr Menon insists I take every day.'

The truth though was simpler. It was because of Jay.

Shalini had once again been threatening to leave as she was completely fed up with Shanthamaaya. But Jay had convinced her that he had to stay till Lalit completed his treatment.

'I couldn't exactly tell her that I wanted to stay here because of you, Juju, right?'

He was sitting on the bed, watching me comb my hair. I recalled a time when I had seen him looking at me in exactly the same manner, as I was untangling my hair, sitting by the window in a small hotel room in Rome. I had never travelled till I met Jay. And apart from going to Pune on a college trip, I had never been outside Bombay.

When Jay asked me to marry him, I had one request.

'I want to see places!' I said.

'Where do you want to go, Juju?'

'Somewhere, anywhere, everywhere.'

And he took me.

~

We were both meandering through a labyrinth of yesterdays, avoiding the existence of tomorrow.

Late one night, before he had to go back to his wife, before his phone alarm rang as a reminder, heralding the dawn of yet another of our dwindling days, our conversation began with me saying 'You remember?' as it often did.

'When we were seeing each other and we broke up for three months, I started dating Rohit and you pushed him off a bar stool though you were also with that tall girl! I forget what her name was, Tanu, Tania?'

'Tara,' he said. 'You were so nasty to her!'

'No, I wasn't. I actually consoled her when she called me once you and I got back together. She was bawling that you slept with her, "used her" were her precise words.'

'What does that even mean! I have never understood this "he took and I gave". Why is it that when it comes to two consenting adults, the man gains and the woman loses? Why don't they both win?'

'And what do they win, what is this grand prize, Jay? A big, fat orgasm?'

'Let's just call it that, Juju, and I want you to make sure you win, multiple times if possible. Like this!'

We both cracked up when he began mimicking me, a parody of ecstatic faces and silly moans that belonged only in porn movies.

I didn't ask him what the future held for us, though I often lay beside him thinking about my role as 'the other woman'.

Was that the right term? When do you start becoming the other woman – is there a protocol? After the first fuck, or a week, a month? I didn't know. I had never slept with a married man before.

What did the future hold for me aside from meeting Jay surreptitiously, lying to my family, lonely birthdays and hurried matinees? I would switch places with Shalini and wait, I suppose the way she used to, for him to abandon his wife.

From the things he said it was clear that life with her was far from ideal.

'Even my mother says I have gone from the frying pan into the fire.' Though it wasn't pleasant to be compared to a Prestige non-stick pan, I could console myself that she had found someone else even less worthy of her precious son.

Jay's father, a laid-back, good-natured man with the same light eyes as his son, had taken a liking to me. Perhaps he felt a kinship, because I soon realized that he was also an outsider like me, hovering around the tight unit that comprised his elegant wife and her beloved son.

At a family gathering, noticing my mother-in-law's disdainful glances, he smiled ruefully at me. 'Don't worry about her, she will get over it. You know, for a while she took him to weddings all over the world arranging for him to bump into appropriate Sindhi girls. London, Udaipur, Thailand, you name the destination wedding spot and she would drag him along, a black suit and an embroidered sherwani in hand.'

He laughed. 'She was trying to make him spontaneously fall in love with "our kind", she would say. His mother was always worried that he would bring some blonde girl home like he used to in his university days. I used to tell her technically Sindhi girls are all frizzy blondes too, but now with you at least she can't complain of that.'

A year after we were married, Dad, as I had begun to call him, passed away. I missed him the most at gatherings at my mother-in-law's art gallery, where the mother and son would wield words like impressionism, cubism and pointillism, as if they had eaten a Sotheby's catalogue for dinner the previous night and were now throwing up on each other.

Trying to change the topic, and get a few laughs, I once said, 'The only word I know that rhymes with these is jism,' only to be rewarded with identical condescending expressions.

Not good enough for his world, for his mother, for him. This was a constant refrain within my head.

I kept trying to please him, trying to prove that no one could ever look after him better. As if I had been hired as a nanny to lay out matching socks, make sure teeth were brushed and meals nutritious. I would fulfil every need, I thought, till there was no space for anything else.

But there is no such thing as complete fulfilment, as I eventually discovered. Even particles of matter are made up of swirling empty spaces.

With Shalini, there seemed to be even more gaping holes. 'It's exhausting to be with someone so young,' Jay complained.

'I am also almost a decade younger than you, Bibet.'

'She is eighteen years younger, Anshu, and if I had to spoon-feed you, then trust me, and you have seen it yourself, here I am bottle-feeding.'

We spent hours each night, spooned together, his leg over my hip. The seven years apart expunged, though its traces were visible. In the way he had to leave my room before dawn, in my refusal to acknowledge, to ask, if he was still doping her with sleeping pills, in the distance we maintained publicly, though I am certain I was not nearly as discreet as I thought I was being.

Over lunch one day, after laughing at one of Javed's jibes at his partner, Vivaan asked Anil, 'How are you still with this man?'

He shrugged. 'Who can explain why one person becomes more important than the many we meet in our lifetime? I only know I still feel the same way about him that people feel when they bring Ganpati to their house.'

Javed retorted, 'So kindly enlighten me, in your opinion am I a plump elephant or a God?'

I blurted out, 'I feel the same way.'

'About me?' quipped Javed.

I shook my head, embarrassed, but still grinning. Being with Jay again, I was unable to contain my happiness – pinholes of joy leaked out of me, in my smiles, the swing in my step, the glow in my skin.

15

She was sitting on the brick wall, facing the lake. It was not like her to miss any classes. Usually she was the first one in the pavilion.

'Jenna,' I called out, 'why did you skip class? Achha, come quickly! Let's get breakfast, I am bloody starving as usual.'

She turned towards me. Her pale eyes were red. She seemed jittery, disoriented.

'Are you all right? What is it?'

She put a hand over her face, her fingers moving in a rocking motion, massaging her eyelid, her eyebrow.

The breakfast bell rang but she didn't move.

I was alarmed. She had a peculiar, battered expression on her face.

'What happened? Are you feeling ill? Come, let's go to the clinic, let Dr Pillai see you.'

She shook her head.

'What's wrong?' I asked again but she did not respond.

I sat by her side, watching her, wondering what had happened.

There were little boys bathing on the other side. Their laughter travelled across the lake, mixed with the sound of birds all around us. Jenna's legs were hanging off the wall, one moving rapidly like it was a metronome setting the tempo to an orchestra of anxiety.

When she finally spoke, it came in a gush.

Lalit's sense of entitlement had always been like the hooting of the siren on top of a politician's car, one that speeds through traffic lights and pushes its way through crammed spaces.

Jenna said he had kissed her a few days ago. She had let him because she felt guilty. 'Because he was, had been, kind to me and I was trying not to be rude. I don't know if it makes sense.'

Last night, he screwed her. Her face pushed against an old armoire, pressing against it with each thrust. Her unwillingness evident but discounted.

'I felt sick but I didn't do anything to stop him.'

'You didn't tell him you didn't want to, Jenna?'

'I did, but I don't know if I said it strongly enough.'

I wanted to shake her. How stupid could she be! Why in the world had she been sitting next to him night after night watching movie after movie? I had warned her about Lalit but she had never taken me seriously. What did she think was really going to happen?

An instant later, I realized I was doing exactly what we had been doing to each other for centuries, what Jenna was in fact doing now, blaming ourselves, blaming other women. Why was she out so late? Why was she wearing that? Why was she drinking so much?

Blame is a bullet that the world fires at an already wounded victim.

Jenna pulled her legs up, holding her knees against her chest. Her eyes fixed on the other side of the lake. She had been dry. He had had to use his saliva for lubrication. A churning in my gut. I felt nauseous listening to her. She continued, her voice was flat now, like she was reading aloud a page from someone else's diary, disconnected.

The slimy, sticky ejaculate he wiped off with her grey underwear later.

She jumped off the wall. I hurried after her, my heart breaking for the vulnerable young woman who I wished I could have protected better.

'Jenna, I don't know what to say to make this any better, but I'm here for you, whatever you need.'

She turned towards me fleetingly. Her skin was like

tracing paper pulled tight on to her bones, a faint network of blue veins visible in the hazy morning light. A nod of her head. I didn't know if that merely meant she had heard me or if it was a dismissal.

Dr Menon was not in the clinic. I waited for him, watching the concentric ripples the rain was creating in the dank pond, while I drank cup after cup of warm dosha water from my thermos. A mundu-clad man was hurrying down the mossy stone steps, his face obscured by an umbrella, and I jumped to my feet, hoping my wise friend had arrived. But it was Dr Pillai.

With a perfunctory good morning, he pushed open the carved door to the men's section and when he reappeared my ex-husband was with him. Jay's hair was oiled thoroughly, a grainy, gooey pack applied to his face. He was smiling lazily, revealing bits of the yellow face pack that had got stuck on his teeth.

'You remember that ad, Vicco Turmeric cream, I feel like the bride in that one. What was the jingle? Haldi ka ubtan something, right?'

'I don't remember,' I said, cutting him short. 'Jay, I have to talk to you alone. This afternoon?'

'Now what happened? How have I wronged my Juju this morning?'

'No, not about us, about Lalit.'

Jay's face was unreadable under the gooey layer. His

posture didn't alter significantly, but there was a stiffness in the spine, a tilt of the chin that gave an impression of heightened attentiveness.

'What is it?'

'I will tell you, I need to tell you, but I just need some clarity myself. I want to talk to Dr Menon first, see what he thinks, what he feels should be done.'

'Done about what? Anshu, I am asking you again, what the hell are you talking about?'

An attendant walking across the clinic reception, carrying bowls filled with leaves and bottled oil, gave us a curious glance.

'Let me talk to Dr Menon first, please.'

'What nonsense! You behave like he is some sort of messiah, writing down all his banal pronouncements in that diary of yours! This place is just a moneymaking racket, Anshu, and your Dr Menon is nothing more than a ghee-dispensing employee!'

I shook my head. 'That's not true – and by the way, you have gunk all over your teeth.'

Bravado instead of bravery because when he looked at me with his cold grey eyes and said, 'Anshu, stop it! Tell me what happened,' I followed him into one of the relaxation rooms and, finding it empty, sat down on a rattan chair in the corner.

'I am going to repeat exactly what Jenna said to me.'

My ex-husband sat on the mud floor, his back against the grey wall, listening to me intently. Apart from the door opening once and a therapist withdrawing, seeing the room occupied, we were not interrupted.

'Jay, the poor girl looked completely wrecked,' I said finally. Jay, his face pack drying up, cracking in places, reached up and held my hand. My kurta was sticking to my back, the air muggy around us in the confined, windowless space. I could see minuscule, almost invisible, insects on the wooden armrest of my chair.

Jay said, 'Let me talk to Lalit. Trust me, Juju, you don't need to talk to anyone else. I will sort this out.'

~

The kitchen helper was reluctant to part with his precious fruits till I told him that both Jenna and I had been absent at breakfast.

It was a long trudge in the rain to the cottage at the far end of the estate where Jenna stayed. Cradling the umbrella between my neck and shoulder, I swiftly peeled a banana and swallowed it in three bites.

My appetite would often assert itself at inopportune times, in hospital canteens, craving for their bland omelette sandwiches, or during parent–teacher meetings, where I sneaked in chocolate biscuits. Sitting beneath a poster depicting the solar system, the mothers would whisper an array of complaints. 'The school is not helping my child become independent,' one would say while taking out an apple from her bag, biting into it and carefully taking the piece from her mouth and putting it into her toddler's. And out from my bag would come a crunchy Britannia Good Day and go into my mouth, both the three-year-old and I chewing in unison.

I recalled reading in one of Shanthamaaya's library books that pittas tend to overeat when worried or aggravated, trying to douse the acidic discomfort in their stomachs with food.

But Jenna with a typical vata's tendency towards irregular appetites would probably not remember to drink water, let alone eat anything.

She was standing on the open section of the porch, drenched, her hair plastered to her scalp. She wasn't alone.

A loathsome frog croaking in the rain, a rolled-up magazine in his hand, was leaning against the door talking to her.

Jenna, golden-haired like the princess in a Grimm Brothers' fairy tale, where a kiss turns the frog into a prince. A story fed to us again and again in various forms: a righteous woman could make a man shed his bestiality to reveal the noble creature he actually was within. But even this amorphous premise was futile here – this frog was not interested in turning into a prince. Lalit already believed he was one.

I shut the umbrella as I reached the porch and Lalit, his self-congratulatory demeanour in place, said, 'Ah, Anshu, I was just telling Jenna, all our Hindi movies have scenes like this with the heroine dancing in the rain!' When neither of us responded he said, 'Isn't this the perfect weather to have tea and onion bhajias. My Dhonu makes the best bhajias in the world, Jenna, you can't leave India without trying some.'

In an instant I found myself towering over him, my dripping wet umbrella raised like a pointing finger. 'Shut up, just shut up, you fucking pig. I know what you are! I know what you've done. Stop trying to behave like everything is normal. You are not going to get away with this! If I were in Jenna's place, I would go to the police, make a complaint against you, as she bloody should.'

Before he could respond, I pulled Jenna inside the room, my hands shaking as I latched the door. Without thinking whether it was my place, I had decided to occupy the space between her and the world. 'Jenna, why are you still talking to that bastard?' She shook her head with a weary, 'I didn't know he was waiting for me.'

'You are all drenched! You will get sick like this!'

She replied, softly, almost to herself, an emptiness in her voice, 'I should leave, Anshu, go back, go home.'

Was that the answer? Would distance and time help her forget and heal? Or would this trauma turn into an unprocessed memory, piled on top of others, making a dark cave that she would get lost within one day?

'Is that what you really want to do? Run away? Jenna, I've spoken to Jay, we will both help you. You just tell me what you want to do.'

She was still, her eyes downcast.

'I don't think you should let him get away with it, though. You did tell Lalit to stop! He didn't. He continued violating you.'

I put my hand on her shoulder. 'Jenna, don't attack yourself for not being vocal enough, attack the person who deliberately chose not to hear you. You think about it and decide what you want to do, whatever you want, I will be with you.'

Then suddenly a thought. 'The underwear, where is it? Did you wash it?' Jenna looked at me uncomprehendingly, as if I were speaking in an unfamiliar dialect and only when I repeated myself did she reply, 'No, I threw it in the bin.'

'In the bathroom? We should keep it, Jenna, just in case.'

She changed into dry clothes and I persuaded her to eat half a pear, leaving the rest of the fruits on the counter, though I knew they would probably remain untouched. I gingerly opened the door, half expecting to see Lalit lying in wait, but the porch was deserted.

To hell with the no-coffee rule. I headed straight to the Prince. Let the sun rise with caffeine and set with alcohol had been one of my principles when I got divorced, till it got out of hand. I had flouted the main tenet of both the treatment and my common sense in any case – thou shalt not have sex with your ex-husband – so I may as well break a few more.

My head was pounding, in rhythm with the sound of the rain on the restaurant's tin roof.

Mandira, as much as I wearied of her constant, unsolicited interference, was also the one I always turned to for advice.

'Anshu! You have called me just in time. Did you get my message? I'm at Apollo. They are about to wheel me in for the procedure.'

'Oh my God! What happened, Mandy?'

'You know my stupid gall bladder, it suddenly started acting up again last night. Too much pain now, have to remove the whole thing, stones and all. But that's not important. You listen to me carefully. If I don't make it back from this just see that all my things go to my daughter. You know Vicky, my neighbour, his wife died and three months later he got remarried. Now his new wife comes over for dinners wearing the dead one's jewellery! Anshu, promise that you will ensure all my handbags go to my Avni. I couldn't bear to have Ramesh's next wife walking all over Greater Kailash with my Gucci.'

'Stop saying stupid things! Nothing is going to happen to you, you will be absolutely fine. Ask Ramesh to message me with updates, please.'

I would have to wait to talk to my sister properly about Jenna, Lalit and, if I built up the courage, about Jay.

Though I knew what Mandira would say if she found out. That I was worthless, that I had no self-respect to allow myself to be placed in this sorry situation.

16

'Every morning my mother would sit on the bed, in her hospital gown, a turban wrapped around her head, and she would apply her bright lipstick,' Madhu said when I asked her about the red lipstick she always sported.

I only wore pale colours on my mouth, or at least I had ever since I met Jay. A passing comment that he had made in jest, about scarlet lipstick, my wide mouth and the Joker from *Batman*, had made me discard the colour permanently.

We were all standing by the stage, waiting for the Kalarippayattu performance to begin. Jenna had retired to her room after dinner, waving away my offer to accompany her back.

'I asked her about it many times,' Madhu said. '"You are not going out, Amma, why do you put make-up on?"

One morning when we were alone, she finally told me. She said that whenever she felt low, she would put on her lipstick and it cheered her up tremendously.'

Two new arrivals, an elderly couple, stooped and gnarled with age, came shuffling along and greeted us with polite nods.

Madhu smiled back at them, revealing the charming gap between her two front teeth.

She continued, 'Amma said to me, "Madhu, when I put on my red lipstick I am telling myself and the world that I still have hope. Sometimes the only thing we have left is hope. Hope that every tomorrow hurts a little less than yesterday."'

Babaji nodded his head sagely. 'Correct thing, she was saying.'

'This shade, Revlon, Cherries in the Snow,' Madhu said, pointing to her lips, 'was my mother's favourite. Unfortunately she passed away three years ago.'

Babaji, as usual, decided to interrupt us with an ode to the tyrannies of fate. In his deep baritone, he said, 'It was not your mother's time to go, Madhuji. If we had organized a Maha Mrityunjaya puja she would have been saved. That is why I am telling you also to be careful. Your horoscope says you have a bad period starting from August when Saturn will enter your eighth house.'

Vivaan could not resist needling the pompous man. 'Madhu, you have one house in Hyderabad, right?' She nodded. 'Yes, and one in Coonoor.'

'See Babaji, Madhu has just two houses, so if Saturn is entering the eighth house it is definitely not hers.'

Babaji ignored Vivaan. 'Come, Madhuji, we will sit in the front row,' he said, giving us a disdainful look as he led his golden goose carefully away.

'When you talk to Madhu, sometimes she seems so sensible and then the next moment absolutely foolish and gullible. I wonder how anyone can fall for that man's corny mumbo-jumbo,' Vivaan said as we took our seats.

'He is her crutch,' I said, telling Vivaan about a conversation I'd had with my mother a few days ago.

One of my mother's close friends had brought bottles of water from the sewage-laden Oshiwara river to distribute as prasad.

She told Mummy that it was holy water as it had turned miraculously sweet. Apparently hundreds of people were drinking the water and jumping into the river.

'Was it really sweet, Mummy?' I had asked.

'I didn't try it, Anshu! At the gymkhana I only like to take a little Thums Up, that also half a glass only. I don't know what boon Usha got after drinking that holy water, but she did get acute dysentery.'

'Poor Usha Aunty! But really, Mummy, everyone spends so much time and energy on all this religion, superstition business instead of asking themselves if they are limping because of the pain or because of the crutch?'

'Correct, beta! But no crutches and no limping for me! Because as you know, Anshu, after my knee replacement surgery, I am fully pain-free!'

'And then, Vivaan, she started cackling away. I still find it hard to figure when my mother is serious and when she is just trying to mess with my head.'

The warriors marched in, a sea of red sleeveless tunics and short langots. Faces we saw every day, attendants and therapists who now with fierce concentration formed a single line. An elaborate salutation was followed by an energetic demonstration of punches and kicks to a rhythmic drumbeat.

We all had a crutch in some form, I thought, looking at my ex-husband, who was sitting with Lalit in the row ahead. He was mine, wasn't he? Both a sign of my weakness and the source of my strength.

~

A few hours later, there was a different kind of drumming on my door.

My ex-husband strode into my room relaxed, a

laid-back ease to his movements as he sat down on the armchair facing me.

He lit a cigarette, drew in deeply.

'You spoke to him, Jay, what did the arsehole have to say for himself?'

'It's not what you have been told, Anshu. There has been a big misunderstanding. Whatever Jenna may have said to you, it was definitely not one-sided. Do you know that they had kissed before?'

'Yes. She said it had happened once.'

'Lalit said it was on two occasions. He told me about the incidents in detail. Anshu, even I have seen them cuddling up together when we went to their cottage to watch movies. She was always stuck to him.'

'I didn't notice anything the time I joined you guys. She was sitting next to me, in fact.'

I had gone down to Lalit's just once for the 'night show' as he called it. After dinner, he would place his laptop on a stool, and pull in chairs and ottomans to provide seating for his makeshift theatre. But his penchant for double entendres and picking a movie, at least that night, which I think he knew involved heaps of sex had ensured that I did not want to repeat the experience.

'I am telling you, would I lie to you about something like this? I know you don't like Lalit but he doesn't need to force himself on anyone! The poor man was completely taken aback. He had no clue that Jenna was even upset. He said even this morning they were talking to each other on the porch in a civilized way. Until you saw them together and began abusing him, screaming about the police and dragged her inside. Is this true?'

'It wasn't exactly like that.'

'I asked him what happened last night and, Anshu, what he told me, I swear to you, sounds completely genuine. He said, "Jay, I can't understand this. We were up late, talking about everything. The butterfly tattoo on her left arm and the mole on her right thigh, so I go kiss her and she kisses me back. She did say no once, but that's it, not after that." He said that if she had wanted him to stop, he would have. He thought it was just one of those things women say so he continued and she didn't say anything after that.'

'Jay, she said no and that's it. He should have stopped immediately.'

'Really, Anshu?' He pulled me to sit beside him on the bed, his hand on my cheek. 'The first time we had sex, if I remember correctly, didn't you also say no and stop a few times, yes?'

I could recall that afternoon clearly. Worrying about the room being too bright, a shyness that I had not felt with my previous two lovers, trying to discreetly remove my tampon.

'Did you mean it, Anshu? You really wanted me to stop then?'

I looked at him, this man I loved, had probably never stopped loving in the last eighteen years and shook my head. 'No,' I said, 'I didn't want you to stop.'

'And yet, my darling, my Juju, you said no not once but several times. If you didn't want to have sex with Lalit, wouldn't you push him, scream? She didn't do any of that, did she?'

My ex-husband laughed. 'You know what I think? Sometimes you have sex and it doesn't live up to your expectations, so you want to blame someone. Lalit is really not as much a ladies' man as he imagines himself to be. Or maybe this is one way of making some quick money on the side. What do you even really know about her? Didn't you tell me that she also went to Brazil, to a faith healer, some John of God? And that she said she was cured till she had an orgasm in her sleep and her symptoms came back? She seems a bit crazy.'

In a moment of indiscretion, I had told him some personal things Jenna had confided in me, not to mock her, but during an argument about celibacy being part of healing. And now Jay was throwing them back in my face.

I thought about her small, delicate face, the pain in her eyes. 'Jay, I don't think she is the kind of person you are making her out to be. She isn't after money or anything like that.'

'All right, perhaps not money but is she normal in any way? Come on, Anshu, that performance art of hers, very avant-garde and all, but you have to be a bit nuts to do those things.'

Sitting at the Prince, just for kicks we had googled various people. Madhu's Facebook profile picture was of her in a strange leopard-print jumpsuit. Pam had a Wikipedia page and links to her YouTube channel. Tubby Afanasy, who we were all convinced was one of Russia's many oligarchs, turned out to have a food packaging business. We had then arrived at Jenna's website and a video titled Removal of Thorns.

There was Jenna stark naked, balancing on one foot. Rose stems were taped to her body, upside down, the red blooms covering her vagina. She was perched on the edge of a high diving board, over an empty swimming pool, with a horde of people looking up at her.

'Anshu, look, I understand how you feel, I feel sorry for her too but she is clearly unstable. Don't entertain all these fantasies of hers, this inherent desire to play the victim. In life if you order a dish and it's not to your liking, you don't get refunds.'

Was Jay right? What did I really know about Jenna? I had never even asked her why she didn't ever wear a damn bra. But the anguish in her voice had been real, the pain tangible, so solid that I could not discount it.

Let me step away, I thought, the distance would provide some perspective and then I would sit down and talk to Jenna about it all.

17

Jenna was sitting on her yoga mat when I entered the pavilion for our morning class. She looked at me expectantly, a small smile on her face. I nodded and rubbed my eyes like I had just woken up, though I had been awake most of the night.

I took my mat to the other corner of the empty room, by the water dispenser, and when Vivaan walked in, I waved him forward to sit next to Jenna instead. Besides the three of us, Anil and Madhu were also attending the yoga session.

We finished the third series of pawanmuktasana and as soon as Srinivasan finished the last chant of Om, I jumped to my feet, put my mat away and rushed out.

I grabbed the orange that was meant to be my breakfast and made for my room. Then I hid myself there, by the window, my head bent over my yellow diary, making to-do lists, between bites of the tart, sweet fruit, washing it down with fennel-infused water, even though I was certain all its dosha-calming properties were now wasted on me.

Dr Menon had been getting progressively more alarmed at my condition. 'I am perplexed,' he said, his hand on my wrist, 'the treatment is almost over and your doshas are still not in equilibrium. This has never happened, Anshu. I know some patients go to that Prince and eat all sorts of things, but you are not like that. Have you been consuming things from outside, or is it something else?'

I lied. About everything.

~

I met Jay on the way to the gift shop. His hair was damp from the drizzle and pushed away from his narrow forehead. My ex-husband kissed me in the deserted corridor. His eyes wide open, wipers on a windshield, darting right and left.

'I just spoke to Lalit again, you telling him about going to the police, that was something else, Anshu. Just genius. He is still shaking like a leaf.' His pleasure in seeing his mighty cousin squirm was evident. 'He knows though there is no case against him, but I think he is very concerned about any bad publicity. Let him stew in that for a bit and I will finally tell him tonight that it's been handled, that I am making sure nothing happens. But not before he signs those damn papers for me.'

'But Jenna, I haven't spoken to her and I am still not sure—'

He interrupted me. 'There is nothing more to discuss, Anshu, we have been through all this. When does she leave Shanthamaaya, sometime this week, right?'

'Tuesday,' I said, 'the same day as me.'

A cloud of expectant silence hovered about us, till finally I asked, 'Is this over after we leave here, Jay?'

'Don't be silly, Juju, of course not.'

'And Shalini?'

A preoccupied tone, his mind elsewhere. 'What about her? Again you have started your old habit of nagging. We'll see, let the time come. Just chill!'

He patted me on the cheek. 'All right, my beautiful Juju, Shanthamaaya's scratchy powder massage now beckons,' he said and went sauntering down the corridor, his words like the little pill of Aspartame that dieters drop into their tea. Sugary with an aftertaste of bitter fenugreek.

18

There were always bells ringing in my world, slicing the day into pieces with their clamouring. Here, in ghee-filled, rain-drenched Shanthamaaya and back home in my small school with its wooden floors and yellow striped walls.

Monday to Saturday, I sat in my office, looking through the glass partition at all the three- to six-year-olds that came in through the bright blue door, consoling myself that instead of having one child I now had a hundred and twenty-five to look after.

It was still not enough and so I had made a decision. My mother had frozen hair, my sister a frozen forehead, I would also freeze something, so I froze my eggs.

But if Jay and I got back together, they would have to continue lying in the icy container. There would be no sperm to fertilize them. Jay had also been against adoption, claiming he would find it impossible to love anything that was not his own.

'I can't do it, Anshu. Do you want me to raise a child the way I would a hamster? That's the best I could do, I know myself.'

I walked down from my room, entered the busy lunch hall and sat at a table with Javed and Anil. Jenna was sitting with Vivaan at the far end and I gave them a cursory wave.

Through lunch, I kept my head down, barely looking up from the beans on my plate. I wanted to leave the table, run on the damp grass, do something, anything and when Anil complained that he had lost his sunglasses – 'You know the ones I love, the Aviators. Can't remember where I left them, I know I had them on this morning!' – I immediately suggested we go looking for them.

I was glad to have a task to occupy my screeching mind. We walked across the mossy stone path, towards the clinic where Anil last remembered he had had his glasses on.

'My mother always says repeat Jeevan Mama three times and you will find what you are missing!' I said.

'Losing my glasses is one thing, Anshu, but I don't want to look like I am losing my marbles, too!'

'Most of these superstitions have some sort of scientific basis, you know,' Javed said as he grabbed a leaf from a tulsi plant on the side. 'See, it is believed that tulsi is a goddess and that it's disrespectful to chew the leaves, so one should swallow them. The fact is that the leaves contain mercury, which damages our teeth and that's probably the basis of this superstition.'

I said, 'So what do you think is the scientific reason for calling out to Jeevan Mama?'

Javed laughed. 'I have no idea. He must be an old saint or something.'

'Let's just try it!' Anil said as he looked up at the cloudy sky and yelled out, 'Jeevan Mama! Jeevan Mama! Jeevan Mama!' and just as I was about to say 'Look out!' he promptly stumbled into a heap of cruddy elephant dung.

'Well, there,' Javed told him, 'Anshu's mother was right, it worked and you did find something. And in this case, can I add finders keepers!'

~

I spent the day tagging along with them, taking a cooking class, though I had not enrolled for it earlier. I took pictures of Anil balancing various vegetables on his head, an eggplant, an oversized pumpkin.

The rain meant that our daily walk and feeding the fish programmes were cancelled. We were all shepherded into the library for an evening of games.

Vivaan, Jay, Shalini and Lalit were playing carrom.

Vivaan captured the queen and looked at me with a smile of triumph from across the room.

For a moment I had a glimpse of an alternate reality. One where a man could be happy with me without my attempts at constantly trying to please him.

A few days ago, he had come to my room before dinner to lend me his phone charger. Mine had rolled over dead that morning.

'A kiss, milady, in exchange for my electrifying services,' he had said wryly.

I kissed him on his cheek, his beard tickling my nose, a laugh bubbling in my throat. 'I am old enough to be, well, if not your mother, then a grand old aunt at least.'

My mother had seen his picture on my Instagram page and had wanted to know if he was single and from a good family.

'Leave it, Mummy, I am not interested.'

'Not for you, Anshu, he is too young! For Jyotsna's daughter I was thinking.'

Vivaan stood looming over me. 'Anshu, when we get out of here, let me take you out. An old bottle of wine and a brand new man, it's a good combination. Consider it a dying man's last wish,' he said in a mock dramatic manner, making me smile.

'Stop saying these things. You are not dying, it's in remission, you told me yourself.'

'Anshu, we all come with expiry dates. The only difference between ours and those of milk bottles you see on supermarket shelves is that theirs are printed on their lids and ours are flying in the wind.'

'Vivaan, come sit here.' I patted the only place where we could sit together in my room, the antique bed.

'I absolutely adore you but I am involved with someone right now and—'

'With your ex-husband?' he interrupted me.

Looking at my startled expression he said, 'I can see the way you two behave around each other.'

'It's complicated, we have a long history together, Vivaan. He has been such a large part of my past.'

'Gandhiji always said, Anshu, if you keep turning and looking behind, all you will get is your old pain in the neck back.'

Before I could respond, he raised his arms in surrender with a laugh. 'All right, he didn't! But he should have, right?'

~

Discarded black umbrellas, a frangipani in Javed's buttonhole, Jay leaving the dining hall with Lalit. My eyes darted, trying to spot Jenna, but she was missing from the dining room.

'I haven't seen her since lunch,' Vivaan said when I asked him as we trooped into a room in the main building to hear Dr Pillai's lecture.

'Should we go and check on her, Anshu?'

I was conflicted. Wanting reassurance that she was fine – and dreading having to speak to her about Lalit.

'Perhaps she wants to rest,' I said. 'I left fruits in her room yesterday, so she must have just had that for dinner.'

Dr Pillai was a good orator with decidedly bizarre concepts. That night he chose to enlighten us about how people could produce superior babies with the aid of garbh sanskar.

'But they have to be conceived by purified parents who copulate at a time dictated by planetary configurations and follow the correct diet, very similar to what you are all eating here now,' he proclaimed.

When the lecture ended, Javed pulled Anil under the umbrella with a sarcastic 'I think Dr Pillai's parents must have conceived him during a lunar eclipse!' and they began the short walk back to their cottage by the botanical gardens.

The steps creaked under my feet as I walked up to my room. The air was oppressive, a musty smell that the lemon oil failed to mask in the humidity.

My eyes were heavy with the need to sleep but I

couldn't lie down. I sat by the window watching the courtyard fill with water. Indecision, a tight feeling in my gullet, a dry morsel stuck in between, unable to bring it out or push it down. Trying to read, I lost my place again and again till I finally made up my mind.

I had to go check on Jenna. Sleep, my enemy, would be looking for the slightest signs of alarm within my consciousness and would use my anxiety as an excuse to flee the entire night.

I tied my hair into a tight plait and set off into the dark, windy night, hoping the umbrella wouldn't collapse on the way.

The stone pathway was dimly lit. I would have to hurry back as all the garden lights were switched off by 11 p.m. My right arm and shoulder were already drenched even under the umbrella.

I crossed the clinic, the lotus ponds, all shadows and outlines.

I could see Jenna's cottage from a distance, the light illuminating the porch.

Three figures in white. Even from a distance I could see that Jenna looked distraught. My ex-husband stood on one side and Lalit on the other. Lalit was holding her arm, talking to her intently, inaudible in the rain.

I walked faster, my jute slippers were wet, muddied, biting into my feet. Jenna saw me, she took a step forward.

Lalit, following her gaze, turned and she pulled her arm from his grasp.

I saw it happening as I rushed towards the porch, like pages from a flip-book. Her left foot slipped on the wet tile, then the right, and off the porch she fell. Backwards from 90 degrees to 75, 50, 10, till finally her head touched the mossy stone courtyard, with barely a sound.

I began running, my feet skidding on the stone path.

The porch was not very high, six feet from the ground at the most. I waited for her to get up, willing her to move.

Her eyes were shut, the rain diluting the blood trickling out of her into pink puddles. She lay there unmoving.

The two men began talking at once, but I couldn't hear them over the sound of the wind. There seemed to be a large gash at the base of her head. I put my hand on her pulse, the rain and my panic making it difficult to sense anything. Was she breathing? Did she have a heartbeat? I couldn't tell.

'We need to get her to the main building, she needs a doctor,' I screamed.

The next half-hour went by in what seemed like minutes. Dr Pillai was on duty that night. His expression of perpetual annoyance was replaced by concern while examining Jenna. An ambulance would have taken too long to come from Thangam hospital, thirty-five kilometres away. We got into his white Maruti, though he first carefully covered the back seat with towels to protect it against bloodstains.

Jenna was still unconscious, breathing. But her pulse was weak, Dr Pillai had concluded, after his examination. 'How did she fall?' he asked, driving on the deserted, potholed roads. 'She slipped down the stairs,' Jay replied swiftly.

19

The chair was unsteady, its legs uneven. The tiny rocking motion gave me the feeling that I was on a boat. The hospital had provided me with a blue kurta pyjama to replace my wet clothes. My underwear was still damp. I should line it with some tissue paper, I thought, or risk a bout of thrush. A fluorescent light was repeatedly blinking on and off, the flickering hurting my eyes.

They had wheeled her out, after the scan, straight to the ICU. There had been a flurry of Malayalam between Dr Pillai and the doctors.

'What are they saying, what has happened to her?'

'Contusion with intracerebral haematoma,' Dr Pillai said.

'There is bleeding within the brain tissue. Now it all depends on how much blood collects, and whether the bleeding continues. They are going to monitor swelling inside the skull also carefully. If it increases, she will have to undergo surgery. Right now, we can't say anything.'

He was ready to leave with the three of us. 'There is nothing you people can do sitting outside.'

'I would like to wait,' I said.

Jenna had no one here and despite the weeks we had spent together, I did not know who to reach.

Lalit stood up and I noticed smears of blood on his forearm. Her head had been in his lap during the car journey. Jay tugged at his cousin. 'Wait,' he said.

This took me by surprise. My ex-husband was very uncomfortable in hospitals. He was not in the hospital room when they brought me back the morning of my termination.

'He has gone home to get his toothbrush,' his mother had said when I opened my eyes and asked for him. 'Jay hates hospitals, even when his father was ill, you know he found it difficult to be there. Whenever he gets stressed, he brushes his teeth. It's the way he used to always comfort himself even as a child. It's an old habit. See how worried he is about you.'

'Worried about you, but has left to go put a pacifier into his own mouth, wah!' my sister said when we were alone in the hospital room.

Jay got me a cup of warm, sweet tea. He sat next to me, silent at first, and then put his hand on my shoulder. 'Anshu, you were there, you saw it was an accident.'

Lalit butted in, 'I was just trying to explain to her that it had all been a misunderstanding. But she started crying, becoming hysterical. I was trying to calm her down when you came, Anshu, ask Jay. I think we should sue Shanthamaaya! How can the cottage porch be without a railing, so careless, anyone can fall off!'

Jay, ignoring his cousin's blubbering, led me to one side of the white-tiled corridor. We passed slumbering relatives stretched out on the floor in between the rows of chairs.

'Juju, all you have to say if anyone asks is the simple truth. We were all talking and she slipped, lost her balance and fell. Nothing more, nothing less. What happened before has nothing to do with it.'

'I won't lie, Jay.'

I was finding it increasingly difficult to concentrate. I was slurring my words. This happened to me often when I was drunk and sometimes when my insomnia was at an extreme, as it had been lately.

I wish I had gone to check on her earlier. I wish I had not abandoned her. 'Star light, star bright, I wish I may, I wish I might, have the wish I wish tonight.' Fragments of a half-remembered nursery rhyme ran through my mind. A muscle in my arm kept twitching. Nerve impulses as discombobulated as I was.

'I am not asking you to lie, Juju. But think about it carefully, there may be an inquiry, I don't know, maybe the police will come tomorrow and talk to all of us. The truth is she fell, Anshu, isn't it? She wasn't pushed. That's all there is to this story.'

His voice seemed far away. Hazy. I was groggy now that the jolt of adrenaline had worn off.

'Jay, you go now, I just want to sleep for a few hours.'

Walking back towards the chair, I glanced at Lalit. 'Go,' I said, waving my hand brusquely, 'and take him with you.'

But Jay didn't leave me, he sat down once again. 'Listen to me, if she' – a hesitation, as he searched for an innocuous term – 'if something happens to her and you have gone and said any nonsense, it will be a case of accidental manslaughter. What do you think, only Lalit will be implicated? Me, Juju, I will be an accessory to this. They will put me away as well. Is that what you want?'

Fear is an animal that sits dormant in your belly until it gets thrown a morsel suited to its taste buds. I could feel anxiety building up, which I knew I was going to chew on and pick at incessantly.

He held my hand, rubbing it, the thin gold band that he had given me years ago chafing against my skin.

'Our future is at stake, our life together. I love you, my Juju, please don't wreck all of this. It was an accident, you saw it yourself. It could have happened at any time, to anyone.' He paused, looking at me carefully. 'As soon as we are home, I am going to tell Shalini that it is over and then it's you and me, the best team in the world like you always said.'

He rubbed my head. 'Juju, please. Promise me you will just tell them that you saw her slip and nothing more.'

In the next hour that he sat beside me, talking to me, I finally agreed to do as he asked, out of fear, or was it sheer fatigue? I was unclear, but I accepted his truth as mine.

~

I am taking new parents for a tour. We have built a brick wall. It frames a canal. The water is blue-green, filled with turtles. I can't find my shoes. The floor is slushy. A toddler, he has my shoes, he is throwing them in the canal. They are in the water now, heels, they hurt my arches but I need them. There is a diving board. I balance at the edge. I lift my arms. I look down. It's not a canal, it's a dark well. I can see a red bucket at the bottom. I am going to jump.

I could feel my legs jerking in my sleep, moving rapidly

as if I was running, slicing through the air, finally waking me up.

I walked to the nurse's desk. 'Bed no. 4, any updates?'

The nurse replied wearily, 'You ask doctor, he will be here at ten.' I had asked her the same question repeatedly but she had not been forthcoming with any sort of reply, claiming that she was authorized only to talk to relatives about the patient's condition.

I was sticky and dirty. A shower, a change of underwear would do me some good. Jay and Lalit had left hours ago while I sat in my wobbly chair, my eyes burning, my mind ticking away in unison with the clock over the nurse's station. I did not know when I had fallen asleep.

'Taxi please,' I asked, 'to take me to Shanthamaaya Sthalam and then wait there for thirty minutes to bring me back.'

She said she would call one for me. It would be here in twenty minutes.

I needed to use the bathroom. 'Left down the corridor,' said the nurse.

The toilet was clean but the flush wasn't working. I washed my hands at the sink. A scratch on my cheek, a dishevelled bun, pallid skin, the mottled mirror looked back at me disdainfully. 'Who is this odd-looking woman, I don't recognize her,' it seemed to say.

Lately when I had caught a glimpse of myself

unexpectedly, my features devoid of both the slight tilt to the right and the smile crafted for photographs, when I was a phantom crossing store windows, a ghost in the rear-view mirror, I found it hard to recognize myself as well.

But that day it was more than just the battering of time, there was an expression held within my eyes, a cast to my mouth that had nothing to do with gravity.

If someone came inside the bathroom and asked me, 'Who is this woman in the mirror, what does she believe in, what are the values she lives by?' I would be unable to answer.

~

I walked towards the canteen with the lone man, mop in hand, trying to obliterate the stench of sickness and despair with phenyl.

I had not carried any money. A glass of tap water was all I could ask him for.

He smiled obligingly and on his way back he kindly switched on the overhead fan for me. The sudden draught swept the paper napkins off the table. I bent down. Picked them up. Put them back on the table, using the sugar pot as a paperweight.

~

The day my marriage ended, napkins had gone flying off the table as well. Strange what the mind chooses to hold on to, three stubs in a crystal ashtray, bits of ash on the mahogany table.

I had walked up to the window, pushed it open. The napkins, the disposable pieces of our domestic life, had flown up in the air, then fallen to the floor.

'I went to the airport to fetch you, Jay. The Calcutta flight landed at five. I waited an hour. You didn't come out,' I said to him as I picked up the napkins nervously.

He hadn't been to Calcutta at all. Instead, he had been holed up in one of the forty-four suites at the Taj Mahal Hotel with his mistress and the view of the Arabian Sea for company. Money opens doors and mouths. Mishra, his driver, was like a vending machine, I discovered. I fed him tokens and the ice-cold truth tumbled out.

Jay had earlier passed off the party picture on Facebook as an event he had to attend because of a new client, Monty, who had brought along his mistress, the girl in red by his side.

Jay was good at making up stories – and he built an elaborate nest of lies around the fictitious Monty and his quest for finding happiness amidst a horde of escorts.

'Can you imagine,' Jay said to me, 'Monty says the Russians are the worst! When he brings one home and after they are done he has a rule. When he goes to the bathroom, his lady friend must stay in bed and keep clapping.'

A short laugh and he continued, 'He says as long as he can hear the sound of the clapping he knows their hands are occupied; otherwise, money, silver, phones – everything they find – all go straight into their enormous handbags. That girl? In the photograph? I don't even know her name, Juju. Monty had asked me to get her a drink, that's all. I won't be surprised if she is an escort too, though Monty was drunkenly proclaiming he was in love with her.'

But that day Jay, who had always used lies as if they were nothing more than bubble wrap to bundle around things to stop them from breaking, gave me the truth.

His grey eyes were opaque, like the marbles we used to play with as children. He said he was tired 'of the air of gloom and doom you carry'.

He expected more from life than what I was offering.

'You have stopped taking an interest in me, in what I need.' His manner had been distant, almost official. As if I were his secretary and he was dictating a letter, ticking off a catalogue of defects in an unsatisfactory vacuum cleaner and asking for a replacement.

At the very end he said that he felt a lightness. 'A sense of relief, to be honest, that you know now. You will be better off without me, happier, and perhaps so will I.

Shalini' – and that was the first time I heard her name, a word that would soon start running on the treadmill of my mind endlessly – 'she makes me feel alive again. If you love someone, won't you want them to be happy? Be glad that I have finally found something to look forward to in my life.'

A marriage doesn't end with lawyers and courts. It dies when two people in the aftermath of shocks and jolts put the defibrillator away, realizing that all this while they had been trying to revive a corpse.

'We tried,' he said, 'but sometimes things don't work out. I have spoken to Mom, she also thinks it's best we do this quickly and amicably.'

And just like that, after having performed endless pirouettes of solicitousness around him, like the serviceable, disposable napkins, I too plummeted to the ground.

20

The taxi driver honked outside Shanthamaaya's arched wrought-iron gates.

The watchman shuffled up to the car, peeked inside and said 'Namaskaram' just the way he had when I arrived. Was it just twenty-six days ago? It felt like a year, time slowing down under the influence of a greater force. I had a long shower, pulled on a pair of trackpants, put my wallet, my credit cards and my phone in my handbag.

It was drizzling again, I could see the rain from my window. I could see her. Shalini, sitting alone at the breakfast table.

Jay wanted me back. And wasn't that all I ever wanted, him wanting me? It would be Shalini's turn to tumble and fall. She was young. She would recover. I doubt if she had spared even a fragment of a thought for me.

I walked back to the foyer and Surya, the receptionist, called out to me, 'Anshu madam, Dr Pillai said to call him.'

She quickly dialled his number for me and handed me the landline.

'Good morning, Anshu,' he said. 'Good news, I have just spoken to Dr Panicker at Thangam hospital. Jenna regained consciousness at night only and also the swelling is down now. They are saying she should be fine but they want to keep her under observation for the next few days.'

'Thank God! Thank you so much, doctor, thank you for everything.'

I disconnected the phone. My heart racing. 'Surya, please tell the taxi to wait for five more minutes, I'm just coming back.'

I wanted to tell Jay the good news. Jenna was going to be all right. The dread that had filled me from the moment I saw her fall from that porch began to dissipate. All my fatigue and weariness disappeared. I walked briskly down the corridor looking for Jay and then I saw him.

He was sitting on the steps leading to the dining area, his back towards me. Talking to his wife, laughing at something she was saying. My ex-husband then bent down and very gently kissed her on the forehead and said, 'Yes, my Juju.'

Juju. A word that I thought belonged only to me.

'Jay,' I said, standing three feet behind him. He moved abruptly, a start that he immediately cloaked within a laugh.

'I want to talk to you.'

His wife gave him a swift glance, a question and a warning all bundled up in one.

'About Jenna!' I said.

'Yes, how is she?'

'That's what I came to tell you. I am leaving for the hospital. Dr Pillai just called. He said she is conscious and should be fine soon.'

'Oh good, what a relief,' he said with a smile.

My voice was flat, cold.

'My taxi is waiting, I have to go,' I said, walking briskly down the corridor.

He got up to follow me, his footsteps echoing along the long passage. Hurried feet, long strides, till we were walking alongside each other.

'You remember what we spoke about yesterday, right? You are the only one who can do this, Anshu. Make sure she doesn't unnecessarily drag Lalit or me into this. I will ensure that Lalit pays all her medical bills, even her Shanthamaaya stay or whatever she wants. But you don't tell her all that, you just see what she says first.'

I didn't respond.

'Why aren't you saying anything, Juju? Why are you behaving like this? Is it because I gave Shalini a kiss on her forehead, for God's sake?'

Juju, perhaps it had always been a term he used easily, the way Khurana Uncle used 'dear', and I was the one who had elevated it. A commonplace stone that I had placed on a shrine.

'I have to get out of this smoothly, you understand. I have to make sure I handle Shalini properly.'

'Yes, you have to handle her and Jenna and me,' I said. 'Have you ever thought, Jay, why using objects and people in a way that causes damage is called manhandling? And there is no female equivalent like womanhandling?'

He looked at me sharply, opened his mouth to say something and then changed his mind.

After a short while he said, 'Just manage this please, Juju, don't let me down.'

I could feel a strain on the left side of my neck, a tightening at the base of my head. With experience, I knew that I would soon have a pounding headache, which would pull at my eyes, like a hand clawing at it from the inside.

Some illusions have a long, lingering death, but mine had just been in a car crash, passengers flung out of the windshield in an instant.

It hurt, the banality of what I had thought was a special

endearment, the fact that contrary to what he said he did have a strong bond with his wife. But what had crushed me was the expression on his face. Brief, fleeting, so slight that it would have been lost if I had not been watching him closely, if I had not known him so well. When he heard that Jenna was conscious, he had looked, and there was only one word for it, disappointed.

The world is full of people with their masks on and their gloves off. I had been foolish not to have expected Jay to be one of them.

I walked towards the cubbyhole where my confiscated shoes were stored, below the sign that had greeted me as I had entered Shanthamaaya's gates: In order to find yourself, you have to leave the world behind.

Dr Menon and I had stood right here, just a few days after my arrival. I had touched the weathered board, laughing. 'I always set off wanting to find myself, but weeks later discover that all I really want to find now is a cheese burger.'

Dr Menon shook his head, a wobble that could mean yes, no, or anything in between and said, 'I have been asking them repeatedly to take this down but no one listens to me. This is not the ethos of Shanthamaaya.'

'What, this quote?'

'There is a famous line, Anshu, by Bernard Shaw, you may have heard it, "Life isn't about finding yourself. Life is about creating yourself." And isn't that what we do here, break you down completely, purge you till there is nothing left and then help you create a new way of being.'

Dr Menon, my wonderful, wise friend, was right.

There was nothing to find. There was no key to a vault, where your true, shining self, perfect and gleaming, awaited you.

'We have a second chance,' Jay had said before he left the hospital, 'we have a chance to build a solid future together, Juju, don't spoil it.'

'Life is nothing but a series of blocks, Anshu,' Dr Menon had continued that morning, 'that we put one on top of another, one piece, one choice, stacking it up as we go along. A monument that is unfinished even in death. But if done right, then meaningful all the same.'

His words had brought up a memory of a trip to Barcelona. Of sitting on a roofless tour bus, my neck bent backward, craning to look at Antoni Gaudí's enchanting Sagrada Família, an incomplete masterpiece that still brought the world to its knees.

But what if you gave someone else the power to shift your blocks, rearrange them, change the order, what would you be left with eventually, except a life of someone else's design?

I could have Jay. I knew that if I did as he asked, I

would have a hold over him, just as he would have the upper hand on Lalit.

But I could see what we would be. What I would become.

I barely slept as it is, how would I sleep then at all, with so many deceits pushing against my eyelids?

If you stack up a pile of half-truths what you get is half a pile of lies.

I could see myself watching him snore, thoughts darkening and deepening with the nights. That practised laugh, his ingratiating smile, even those freckled hands, would slowly start filling me with revulsion while I struggled to hold on to a semblance of what I once was.

'I'll handle it,' I said.

I went to the reception and asked Surya to make another phone call from the landline.

The taxi dismissed, I sat waiting by the marble stairs.

The Tata Nano arrived and for a moment I felt disoriented when I saw Dr Menon emerging from the car. A folded newspaper in his hand, he had on a snug purple T-shirt and khaki pants that he wore absurdly high up on his waist and white sneakers.

I had always, and rather foolishly, imagined him wearing nothing else but his cream mundu-jubba even at home.

I walked down the stairs and, for the first time in our

long association, I found myself reaching out to him, hugging him as I wept. For myself, for Jenna, for so many women like us, trained to appease, bending backwards till we find ourselves lying flat on the floor as someone tramples all over us.

My ex-husband had once told me, 'There are no absolutes, things are never right or wrong, they swing in between. People see the truth as a compass but it is in reality a pendulum.'

I gave Dr Menon the truth. I gave him the grey underwear, the one that I had picked out of the bathroom bin and shoved on the top shelf of Jenna's cupboard, and the agitated altercation I had witnessed on the porch. I gave him a pendulum that swung with the might of a wrecking ball as we drove to the hospital to see Jenna.

~

Two days later, I left Shanthamaaya Sthalam.

Vivaan, Anil and Javed came to drop me to the taxi, helping me with my weightless bag.

I was dressed for the airport, a blue T-shirt, a stole around my neck, my jeans, the waistband now loose after all the ghee and purging.

'I'm so tired of these pyjamas,' Anil said looking at my clothes. 'I always tie it so tight that I almost end up peeing in my underpants before I can untie it! Can't wait to get back into my jeans too.'

I knew that a few months down the line mine would be snug once again. Too many Chinese meals would begin undoing some of Shanthamaaya's magic.

'Anil,' I said, 'pyjamas are forgiving in nature, it's jeans that really know how to hold a grudge.'

Vivaan tilted his head and looking at me intently he asked, 'And which one are you, Anshu?'

A reiteration of the games we played in Shanthamaaya: which cartoon characters did we resemble? Which animal? The consensus had been that I looked like an owl, Javed a horse, Jenna a flamingo.

I thought of Jay, not the one trying to appease Lalit and placate Dr Menon in the consulting room, unaware that I was leaving, but the Jay I had known since I was twenty-five. The one who would write me little notes, on hotel stationary and the back of menu cards.

I still had one that said Bristol on one side and on the other, in his untidy handwriting:

My darling wife, I am always looking at you, at all your little details. This morning I realized that you have perfect teeth, has anyone told you that? White, even, with no gaps, you, my Juju, are an orthodontist's delight as much as you are mine.

Never stop smiling my baby,
Love you today, tomorrow, always,
Your Bibet

A silly little note but whenever I read it, it had made me cry.

Lalit had been right that day in the library when he said that I was going back to take second helpings of my favourite dessert. Jay, unfortunately, would always remain my deep-fried gulab jamun, a delicacy from the days gone by when I had an indefatigable constitution but one I could not digest any more.

I hugged my three friends, one after the other. They all smelled the same, the Shanthamaaya smell of sesame oil and ghee that would reek out of our pores for the next few weeks, and I said, 'I will always be a pyjama, I am just going to be one with a shorter drawstring.'

A Note on the Author

Twinkle Khanna is one of India's top-selling writers and the author of two national bestsellers, *Mrs Funnybones* (winner of a Crossword Book Award 2016) and *The Legend of Lakshmi Prasad*. She is one of *Times of India's* most read columnists and has won numerous awards, including India Today Woman Writer of the Year, Outlook Award for Most Inspiring Woman of the Year and Vogue Opinion Maker of the Year. She is the founder of Mrs Funnybones Movies and in 2018 produced the highly acclaimed film *Pad Man*. Khanna lives in Mumbai with her family.

juggernaut

THE APP FOR INDIAN READERS

Fresh, original books tailored for mobile and for India. Starting at ₹10.

juggernaut.in

CRAFTED FOR MOBILE READING

Thought you would never read a book on mobile? Let us prove you wrong.

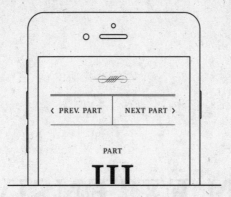

Beautiful Typography

The quality of print transferred
to your mobile. Forget ugly PDFs.

Customizable Reading

Read in the font size, spacing
and background of your liking.

AN EXTENSIVE LIBRARY

Including fresh, new, original Juggernaut books from the likes of Sunny Leone, Praveen Swami, Husain Haqqani, Umera Ahmed, Rujuta Diwekar and lots more. Plus, books from partner publishers and loads of free classics. Whichever genre you like, there's a book waiting for you.

3

DON'T
JUST READ;
INTERACT

We're changing the reading experience from passive to active.

Ask authors questions

Get all your answers from the horse's mouth.
Juggernaut authors actually reply to every
question they can.

Rate and review

Let everyone know of your favourite reads or
critique the finer points of a book – you will be
heard in a community of like-minded readers.

Gift books to friends

For a book-lover, there's no nicer gift than
a book personally picked. You can even
do it anonymously if you like.

Enjoy new book formats

Discover serials released in parts over
time, picture books including comics,
and story-bundles at discounted rates.
And coming soon, audiobooks.

4

LOWEST PRICES & ONE-TAP BUYING

Books start at ₹10 with regular discounts and free previews.

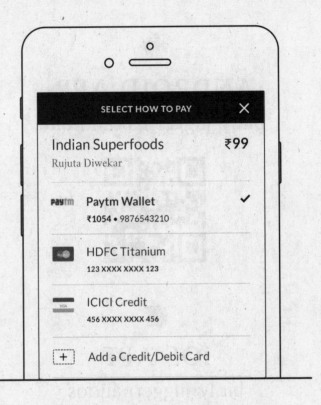

Paytm Wallet, Cards & Apple Payments

On Android, just add a Paytm Wallet once and buy any book with one tap. On iOS, pay with one tap with your iTunes-linked debit/credit card.

Click the QR Code with a QR scanner app
or type the link into the Internet browser
on your phone to download the app.

ANDROID APP

bit.ly/juggernautandroid

iOS APP

bit.ly/juggernautios

For our complete catalogue, visit www.juggernaut.in
To submit your book, send a synopsis and two
sample chapters to books@juggernaut.in
For all other queries, write to contact@juggernaut.in